The Spy Trap

The Spy Trap

By William Gilman

In addition to this startling espionage mystery
this book includes other true stories of the
secret warfare of the FBI today.

WILDSIDE PRESS

The stories contained in this volume
have been chosen by John Shuttle-
worth, editor of True Detective magazine, as the most exciting and mystify-
ing actual espionage cases of the second
world war.

Contents

The Spy Trap

One

THE BEADY-EYED SPY chief known as Nikolaus shifted uneasily. He whispered in German to the little man at his side. "I don't like this—he should have been here five minutes ago."

Ernst Bohm, whose job was to ferret out likely prospects, replied, "I'm sure he will come."

"He's worth waiting for," Nikolaus muttered, "if he can be trusted."

"Absolutely," the other replied. "He is loyal to Hitler, and even more loyal to the jingle of money."

It was a day early in 1938. The two men stood in the shadows near a street corner in Glendale, Queens—in the Long Island section of far-flung New York City. Nikolaus peered uneasily toward other shadows, wondering what they might contain.

It was distinctly unusual for a person as important as Nikolaus, head of the Nazi secret service operating out of Hamburg, Germany, to be exposing himself this much. But he knew that the man, Herman Lang, who lived near by, was worth both the wait and the risk, because it was a matter of the bombsight. Not just any bombsight. But the famous, secret Norden one.

What an accomplishment it would be, what medals he would win, if he could deliver its secrets to Air Marshal Herman Goering! Germany was preparing for her lightning war. That mean air bombing. But dropping bombs wasn't much good unless you hit your target. That's where the bombsight comes in. It's the intricate sighting device that is absolutely necessary for a hit. Its mechanical brain figures out when a bomb should be dropped.

It makes allowances for plane altitude, plane speed

and wind velocity. For instance, if a bomber were flying at 20,000 feet over New York City, and the bombardier wanted to hit City Hall, he'd have to drop his bomb two miles before the plane was directly over the target, and by the time the bomb hit, the plane would be far past the explosion. That's because the bomb doesn't drop straight down, but falls at an angle due to the bomber's speed.

The Nazis had bombsights but nothing, they knew, that could compare with the Norden. It was an American secret. With the turbo-supercharger, it was enabling the Americans to write a new chapter in military aviation. The charger allowed a "flying fortress" to go eight miles up—to fly in the thin air of the substratosphere. And the bombsight made it possible to hit a target from that fantastic height.

In ordinary flanking, you go around the sides of the enemy. The Norden made "vertical flanking" possible—you could go over the enemy, out of sight and out of reach.

Ach Himmel! such beautiful destruction could be accomplished with it! And here it was in the hands of the stupid Americans, those fools who talked about peace and democracy. By every rule of "might makes right" it should be in the hands of those super-warriors of that super-race, the Nazis. Heil Hitler!

And so, shadowy Nikolaus was waiting for Herman Lang. The Nazis had for some time been trying to place an agent in the employ of the Carl L. Norden Co., Inc., whose main office was at 80 Lafayette Street, New York. This company manufactured the secret bombsights for Uncle Sam. Ernst Bohm had finally wormed his way in.

But that's as far as he got. As a mechanic in another department, he got only glimpses of parts of the bombsight, and his itchy fingers never came anywhere near a blueprint showing its secrets. So Bohm was ordered to look around for a trusted employee who could be bought.

Before long, he reported that he had found the right

man. America had been good to Herman Lang, but he preferred Hitler. A native of Germany, and a machinist by trade, he had come to America in 1927. Two years later, he got a job with a tool company making instrument parts for Norden. In 1936, he went to work for Norden as a mechanic, and then was promoted to assistant inspector.

This made him the answer to Nazi hopes. There were five of these assistant inspectors, working under a chief inspector, and the most important of their duties was to go over every finished bombsight to see if it was built according to blueprint specifications. They had all been cautioned that the instrument was a secret one. But Lang was a Nazi and was greedy for money, and willing to sell out his employer and his adopted country.

"He's the only man in the plant," Bohm had told Nikolaus, "who both can and will give us what we want."

And now the "only man" was approaching the conspirators. He was a rangy fellow in his late thirties, with a snub nose and close-cropped head of blond hair. What marked him most, though, was his sad—almost stupid—expression. But Nikolaus wasn't deceived. There was a peasant cunning in Lang's blue eyes.

Bohm spoke in German, "Herr Lang, here is the Dr. Rantzau I was telling you about—the expert in textiles."

"I do not care for tricky talk," the sad-faced man said slowly. "Is your name really Rantzau and do you really want to talk about—textiles?"

Nikolaus replied curtly, "My name doesn't concern you. And you know what I want to discuss. Let us take a walk." He turned to Bohm, "Wait for us here."

The two men walked. "Are you an American citizen?" Nikolaus asked.

"No—but I took out first citizenship papers in 1933."

"Then you must complete the process of becoming an American citizen. Otherwise, they might take your job away from you one of these days. But that can wait until you return from Germany."

[7]

"Then I am going to Germany?"

"Of course! To show us how to make the bombsight."

Lang pondered. "If I go to Germany, I don't want to come back."

"You don't seem to understand," Nikolaus said, "We will pay you well for this—perhaps ten thousand dollars. But that need not be the end. We need men like you in America. You will go back to Norden and report on further improvements in the bombsight."

"Then why should I go to Germany at all?" Lang asked. "I have the plans all in my head. I can sketch them for you."

"All in your head—fine! That makes it perfect. I want nothing on paper. I want you to carry nothing on paper. So there will be no danger. You will simply take a leave of absence immediately. You will explain to friends that you and your wife are going to Germany to visit relatives, or to give your wife medical treatment there."

Lang nodded assent and they went back to Bohm. Nikolaus addressed the latter grimly. "Herr Lang here understands the consequences if he betrays?"

Bohm nodded. "He knows."

And the spymaster—whose real name was Adolf Fritz Ritter, but who was generally known as Nikolaus in the shadowy Nazi spy setup—and by a host of other names ranging from Frank Harris to Dr. Renken—went on his way quite pleased with himself.

His sojourn in America hadn't been entirely a pleasant one. His main job had been to reorganize a foolproof system here, in view of the war that was coming. He had found wreckage and fear, due to a roundup of Nazi spies the Federal Bureau of Investigation had just staged.

Two

THE BRILLIANT WORK of the FBI had been aided by the amateur bungling of the spies themselves. And by bungling in Nikolaus' own office. Much of the spy information had been mailed to a woman in Scotland, who then mailed it on to a man "Sanders" in Germany, who was Nikolaus' assistant, Heinrich Sorau.

But British counter-espionage agents had caught the woman, and the trail from her led back, with one after another of the spies in America falling into the toils of the law.

Berlin had blamed Nikolaus and he, in turn, had given Sorau a tongue-lashing. And the latter had tried to alibi that it was hard to get good spies. Ardent Nazis were usually fools. And non-Nazis professionals always wanted more money, money, money. *Himmel*—didn't they know that by the time Goering, Goebbels and Himmler got through feathering their own nests, there wasn't much left!

At any rate, to save his job, Nikolaus had been forced to risk his own neck in coming to America to set up an efficient spy system. It would have to be highly efficient, he knew, because Director J. Edgar Hoover's FBI had shown itself to be worthy opposition. He was too much a Nazi to admit that the FBI was his equal, of course, but he did see the G-men could give him plenty of trouble.

One of his first tasks was to set up a better pipe-line of information. He planted agents in out-of-the-way places all over the world—Spain, South America, China —whose only job was to receive letters from spies in the United States, and pass them along. In addition to these "letter-boxes," he had key men begin recruiting couriers among the crews of ships plying across the Atlantic.

Meanwhile, in New York City, he lost no time looking up his brother Hans. It turned out to be somewhat of a reunion because Hans was living in an apartment on Riverside Drive with a plump divorcee named Else

[9]

Weustenfeld—who happened to be from the brothers' own home town in Germany, the city of Essen.

Nikolaus lost no time enlisting them.

"We'll send you to South America," he told Hans. "I'll let you know later when and where." Then he turned to Else, "I need you, too. I hear you're a stenographer and a good accountant. Until I get somebody else, I'll have you handle payments to my American agents."

"But won't I get in trouble?" she demurred. "I've become an American citizen."

The spymaster smiled. "That's the perfect combination. That's the kind of agents I want. The Fuehrer demands that everybody born in Germany be loyal to Germany. At the same time, when you're an American citizen, you can get around and do things a foreigner couldn't do."

When Nikolaus had gone, Else said to Hans, "I don't see why he should order you and me around, even if he's your brother. I don't want anything to do with his monkey business."

A look came into the man's eyes she had never seen in the five years she had been living with him: one of fear and hate combined.

"You'll do as you're told," he said, "and so will I. You don't seem to realize that Nikolaus is from the Gestapo. When the Gestapo wants you to do something you either do it—or die."

Else giggled nervously. "I was just kidding, Hans. Of course, I'll help."

Nikolaus covered a good deal of ground during his few weeks in America. And when he sailed back to Hamburg, under the name of "Frank Harris," he was quite satisfied with himself. He had put confidence—and hopes for big money—back into several of his spies. And he had enlisted Herman Lang—if that deal went through, it would be worth all the rest put together.

Meanwhile, a Gestapo agent in New York had been assigned to keep an eye on Lang—to see whether he might not be trying a double-cross. His reports soon indicated that Lang had really taken the bait. And Nikolaus now began awaiting the arrival of the sad-faced man.

Lang had begun by informing friends and fellow workmen that his wife was sick and he was taking her to Germany for medical treatment. The story was accepted. Everybody knew that Lang could afford it. He was making $70 a week and had been working steady for several years.

Then, giving the same excuse, he asked the Norden company for a leave of absence. It was granted.

Over in Hamburg, early in June, 1938, Nikolaus got the flash he had been eagerly awaiting—his New York agent sent word that Lang and his wife had sailed, aboard the S. S. *Hansa*.

When the ship docked at Cuxhaven, Hamburg's port, the sad-faced man seemed almost merry. At last, he was going to set foot on Nazi soil. But he got a shock. His eleven years in America had given him a strange disease —a dislike of being shoved around.

Instead of going through the Customs like other passengers, he and his wife were at once taken into special rooms by Gestapo agents and given a long questioning. Then their baggage was searched minutely.

"Hey, what does this mean?" Lang protested. "I want to see Dr. Rantzau."

"Silence!" he was ordered. "You're in Germany now. And you'll do as you're told."

His wife was kept in Hamburg and Lang was taken aboard a train for Berlin. There, he found Nikolaus waiting at the station.

Lang spluttered with rage over the treatment he had been subjected to. "Am I a prisoner?" he demanded.

Nikolaus smiled. "Certainly not. We were just taking good care of you because you're so precious to us. Come on now, forget what happened. We're going to see some people."

[11]

They drove at once to the headquarters building of the *Luftwaffe*—Germany's air force, and Nikolaus led the way into a private office.

"Herr Beyer," the spymaster said to the uniformed man sitting there, "this is the Norden expert."

Beyer looked at Lang arrogantly, without getting up. "So you claim to have the bombsight secret?"

What with this cool reception, and the treatment he had been getting, Lang turned sullen. "As you wish," he said. "I don't know much about the bombsight. I've only seen some of its parts."

Beyer arose wrathfully and shouted at Nikolaus, "Why bring me a man who works only on parts?"

But the spymaster kept his temper. He turned to Lang and said, "I'm sure you are over-modest. Come now, my friend, and explain to Herr Beyer. Nothing will be too good for the man who gives us that bombsight secret— even a personal congratulation from the Fuehrer. Am I not right, Herr Beyer?"

The other took the cue and turned oily, too. "Certainly. Tell us about yourself, my friend."

Lang was basking now. He began talking. Soon, experts were called in.

He spent three weeks with them, pouring out everything he knew about the Norden bombsight.

Then, as he boasted later, he had a meeting with both Hitler and Air Marshal Goering, the latter telling him that the Norden bombsight was "the most important thing in the world."

He had another meeting with Nikolaus. "You have been very satisfactory," the latter said. "You may now rejoin your wife and enjoy yourselves in our happy country. Visit me before you sail."

The Langs visited relatives in northern Bavaria, and while the traitor loafed around, picking mushrooms and berries, he wondered when he was going to get paid for his treachery.

But when he saw Nikolaus again, before sailing back

to the United States, the latter couldn't say anything definite.

"Our experts are still hard at work building a model of the bombsight. If it works, you'll be paid—never fear. Go back now, expect to hear from us again, keep your eyes and ears open—and remember, you are with us now. The Gestapo allows no resignations. Heil Hitler!"

Some time after Lang's return to the United States, the Norden company required that all of its employees be American citizens. But this didn't affect the traitor Lang, who was back on his old job with eyes open for something more to sell to Berlin—he had followed Nikolaus' orders, and become an American citizen.

Three

BUT THE SPY CHIEFS had their eggs in more than one basket. For example, Herman Lang didn't know Everett Minster Roeder, and Roeder didn't know Lang. Yet they were doing practically the same thing. Roeder, born in New York City, of German descent, had been on the Nazi payroll for a long time. His usefulness to Berlin was obvious—he was an engineer and designer employed by the Sperry Gyroscope Company, at Brooklyn, which was a rival of the Norden company in building special instruments of war. In addition to putting out a bomb-sight of its own, it built automatic pilots for American warplanes, automatic airplane detectors for anti-aircraft batteries and many other secret instruments. We shall hear more of Roeder later.

As months passed, the spy ring kept building up cautiously. Among others, in 1939, it received a new recruit from Europe, the Viennese artist's model, Lilly Barbara Carola Stein, twenty-seven years old, an attractive blonde, formerly a brunette.

It's a toss-up whether she had less brains than morals, because she certainly had little enough of either. But after weeks of coaching by Captain Sorau, Nikolaus' Gestapo assistant, it was felt she wouldn't blunder in the simple tasks assigned to her. One was to mingle in New York society and see what information she could pick up. Another was to act as a messenger, carrying instructions and funds to Frederick J. Duquesne, the soldier-of-fortune who had become Germany's ace spy in America.

Duquesne had been complaining bitterly to Else Weustenfeld, the rings' paymaster in New York, "How can I work if I don't get any money?"

Else had replied she couldn't pay him anything until she was authorized to do so, and had passed the word to Hamburg that Duquesne was getting pretty impatient.

So Lilly Stein was given something to satisfy Duquesne—$500 and a microphotograph of instructions. The latter was a tiny film, the size of a postage stamp. It represented a new method of smuggling messages, developed by the Gestapo. A photograph was taken of a page of writing. Everybody is familiar with the process by which a photograph is "enlarged" into a bigger one. In this case, the opposite was done. The photo was reduced to postage-stamp size. The negative was given to Lilly—the words on it were so small that the negative looked blank. But if it were enlarged, the message could be read again.

While she was being coached, the day for which Germany's spies had been preparing arrived. England called Hitler's bluff. Hitler sent his armies into Poland. A shocked world saw the Nazis plunge civilization into World War Number 2.

German ships scurried to cover in fear of the British fleet. To get Lilly Stein across to America, she had to be sent by a roundabout route. When she arrived in New York late in October, it was aboard the S.S. *Drottningholm,* a Swedish vessel.

Her instructions had been made simple, to match her mentality. They were easy to carry out. She registered at the Windsor Hotel, then sent a letter to Else Weustenfeld in which was enclosed a note signed by Sorau: "I am sending this woman to you. Will you please help her?"

When Else arrived at the hotel, Lilly greeted her with the password, "I bring regards from your friends from *Verden, an der Aller.*"

Else nodded and asked, "What else do you bring?"

Lilly handed over the $500 and the microphotograph. "I am to give them to you and you are to give them to Jimmy Dunn."

A few days later, "Jimmy Dunn" visited Else's apartment, pinched her cheek and said, "What's up, sweetheart?"

When she handed him the money and film, he grinned,

"So Jimmy is becoming useful to them again, is he?"

"Jimmy Dunn," of course, was Frederick Duquesne. But it was only one of his aliases, of which I have counted 41—and they are only the ones I know about. He had the kind of face that was perfect for masquerade. This, combined with his mastery of accents, enabled him, as "Julian Zeller," to be an Austrian; as "von Goutard," to be a German; as Captain Claude Stoughton, to be an Australian army officer, and so on.

In 62 years, he had lived a dizzy pace as a con-man, ace spy, soldier-of-fortune, writer and lady-killer. He was as cunning as he was callous.

He had an impressive head of black hair sprinkled with gray. His face was rugged, seamed, chiseled. He could look like a man who had suffered—like a great composer, or philosopher. His nervous, expressive hands were those of an artist. His smile could melt a stone. And his eyes—dark and bold—were those of a pirate.

But it's impossible to understand this fantastic personality who will play so big a part in this story unless we know something of his past history. Here's how it runs, in brief: He was born in 1877, in the South African Republic. He studied engineering, but when the Boer War came in 1899, he served as a spy against the British.

He was sentenced to a hard-labor term in Bermuda. But eight months later, he smuggled himself aboard a wealthy American's yacht and came to the United States.

He studied military technique in Belgium next, and in 1905 he was an observer-cadet in the Russo-Japanese war. Then he claims that King Leopold of Belgium personally sent him to the Belgian Congo to report on rubber plantation conditions, and atrocities against natives.

He claims he returned to the United States to lecture on behalf of the Paulist Fathers, then he became a New York newspaperman. Another of his claims is that he became a personal friend of the late Theodore Roosevelt through their mutual love of big-game hunting, and often visited the White House.

Four

AFTER MARRYING AND LATER divorcing an American girl, he roamed through South America, then returned to the United States and began promoting inventions, fleecing innocent inventors. But when the first World War broke out, he turned to bigger game. With a chestful of medals he had obtained in a pawnshop, and posing as an Australian army captain, he went around the country collecting "relief" funds—the object of relief being himself. But at the same time, he was working for a German spy ring operating in this country.

In 1918, the British had him arrested in New York, on a charge of murder—for having caused the deaths of three seamen on the British steamer *Tennyson* by the explosion of a bomb placed in a trunk aboard the vessel.

Duquesne put on an insanity act—so effectively that, instead of ordering his extradition to England, the court declared that he was "judicially insane" and he was sent to Bellevue Hospital. When he was later transferred to Matteawan State Hospital, he quickly escaped.

Five months after this, New York police arrested him again, and he was placed in the Tombs, pending an outcome of his case. He tried playing the martyr, proclaiming that "British agents" had kidnapped him, mistreated him and so forth. When that didn't work, he dug back into his bag of tricks and came out—"paralyzed." It was such a good act that he was sent to Bellevue Hospital again. Some Irish Republicans, who thought he was the victim of British persecution, helped him escape for the second time.

He showed up next in Boston. For four years, he ran an advertising and propaganda outfit. Then, he claims, he was publicity man for Joseph Kennedy, recently our Ambassador to Britain—who was then a motion picture executive.

We next find him back in New York, as "Frank de Stafford Craven," writing for motion picture magazines.

In 1932, a new book was published. It was called, "The Man Who Killed Kitchener," and it claimed to tell Duquesne's story of how, in the World War year of 1916, he plotted the sinking of the British cruiser *Hampshire,* with Lord Kitchener aboard—with Duquesne himself being rescued by a German submarine.

When the book appeared, the British did two things. They pointed out that Duquesne was a liar, because they had proof that in 1916 he was in the United States and not aboard any British cruiser. And they had him arrested on the old charges of murder and escape from custody. But he beat the rap, went to work for the WPA a while, and then set himself up again as an expert on inventions. But this was just a cloak for his real business —selling American technical secrets to Germany, which by now was again arming for war—under Hitler this time, instead of the Kaiser.

He was reckless, audacious, cunning—so Nikolaus had looked him up and enlisted him on his American visit. In addition to himself, Duquesne brought into the ring his "assistant"—though she was more of a dupe than anything else. She was Evelyn Clayton Lewis, thirty-six years old, a handsome, artistic woman who dabbled in sculpturing and writing plays. Unlike the others in the spy ring, she came from old American stock. Her family had been in this country 200 years and she was born in Arkansas. Anyway, she had met Duquesne and fallen in love with him. And although she didn't know it at the time, he had full intentions of using her as a messenger whenever he didn't dare show his own face.

Meanwhile, over in Germany, William G. Sebold came ambling into the picture. He came at a very opportune time.

Nikolaus had been looking around eagerly for one very important cog he needed in the American spy machine. He didn't want an actual spy; he had plenty. When he needed was a funnel through which the spy information could reach Germany—a man who would receive and send on reports, and would act as paymaster to the spies and relay their instructions.

He would have to be a contact man. Nikolaus didn't want the spies to know one another any more than could be helped—because if one was caught and began talking, it would be disastrous for all the rest. Nikolaus wanted a man who would know all the spies and act as their clearing house—and be tough enough to keep his mouth shut when danger came.

Sebold, who had served two years with the German army in the first World War as a machinegunner, was certainly tough enough. He was a six-foot, two-hundred-pounder who walked like a bear, with a heavy, flat-footed trudge. But even though his shoulders were broad and his fists were ramrods, he didn't have the appearance of a pug. He looked more like what he actually was—an honest working man. His face was stolid, and his light-brown hair was combed carefully.

And when the first two Gestapo agents began questioning him as if he were a criminal, his reaction also was that of an honest workman—to send his fists crashing into their arrogant faces.

But he restrained himself. He explained that, although born in Germany forty years ago, he had been an American citizen for many years. He had just landed in Hamburg from the steamer *Deutschland,* having come from New York. He explained that he had just gone through an operation for stomach ulcers and thought it would be a good idea, while he was unable to work, to look up his relatives in Germany.

He didn't explain that another reason for looking up his relatives was to see if there was any way of getting them out of Germany, in case they had as little use for Hitler as he had.

The Gestapo men became really interested when, answering their questions, he said that he had been working for the Consolidated Aircraft Corporation plant at San Diego, Calif. But when they tried to learn more, he shut up like a clam, saying he didn't know much about it, because he was just a laborer, not an engineer.

They took down the Ruhr Valley address where he was going to visit his mother, and let him amble away.

Sebold proceeded to enjoy the family reunion, and forgot about the Gestapo—until three weeks later. Then he got a letter signed by a Gestapo official named "Dr. Gassner." The latter asked for an immediate meeting with Sebold.

Sebold was worried, and his phlegmatic face twisted with a fierce expression—one of his habits when something was bothering him. It was plain enough to him that the Gestapo wanted still more from him. He decided not to worry his family, and to do nothing.

Five days later, he got another letter from Gassner. This time, the Gestapo man wasn't asking; he was demanding a meeting. "You do not seem to realize that you are now in Germany," he wrote. "Beware of forcing us to apply pressure."

Again Sebold didn't reply. A week later, a man came to the house and said he wanted to see Sebold—alone.

He was a thin, weasel-faced man. "I am Dr. Gassner," he said. "Why haven't you written me?"

"Because I saw no need."

Gassner smiled thinly. "We've handled people like you before."

Sebold laughed. "Who are you trying to scare? All right, Gassner, what is it you want to know so badly? Why am I so important?"

The Gestapo man nodded. "Now you're talking like a sensible man. I want to know all about that aircraft plant where you were working."

"That's what I thought," Sebold said. "Well, I don't like this sort of monkey business. If you want to find out so badly, go to California yourself—it's a free country."

Gassner picked up his hat. "I shall leave you now. But I will be back—I, with some others—unless you write first, explaining that you're willing to cooperate.

You do not seem to understand our new Germany, Herr Sebold. Perhaps you are planning to escape. Perhaps you can succeed. But do remember that your mother, your two brothers and your sister will be here. I haven't time to explain to you what their lives will be like in the concentration camp. But they will wish they were dead, and so will you. Good-by, Herr Sebold."

Sebold paced the floor, clenching and unclenching his fists.

He wasn't the first to hear such sinister words from the Gestapo—the murdering, torturing secret police commanded by Heinrich Himmler. The Nazis proclaimed that everybody in the United States of German birth or descent belonged to them. The fact that most such American-Germans were loyal to the United States meant nothing to Berlin. It believed in the power of threat.

And that was how its spy ring had been built up— from crooks, and professional spies, and Nazi crackpots —and fear-stricken cowards who wanted nothing to happen to themselves or their relatives.

But William Sebold was of a different caliber. He represented the best type of American-German—loyal to Uncle Sam. Even more important, he feared no man. That's why the Nazis failed to understand him.

As he paced the floor, a rage grew in his heart. He wanted nothing more than to punch into insensibility the bullies who were forcing him to choose between his loved ones on one side of the scale, and his country on the other. It was no easy choice to make. It's all too easy to think first of yourself and your kin. But Sebold was no ordinary person. There was something heroic in him. He was not afraid of death. He had what the fighters call "guts."

He knew he would have to work fast, and secretly. He told his mother he was going to spend a few quiet days hiking in the countryside.

Shortly after midnight, he crept out of the house and stole through the shadows. Soon he was walking rapidly down a road. Five miles farther, he came to a small town where he boarded a bus.

His destination was Cologne, where he knew there was an American Consul.

Sebold showed Gassner's letter to this official and explained what had been going on. "If you are willing," he said, "I would like to agree to work with them—and then turn over everything I learn to the FBI. I don't know much about undercover work, I suppose, but maybe I can be of use."

"There's nothing I can do," the Consul said. "You're in a bad spot, and I sympathize. I'd like to have copies made of those letters, though. And you might drop back in a couple of days for the originals."

Sebold went away despondently. He had expected a more energetic response. He wondered if perhaps the Consul suspected that he was really a Gestapo man trying to worm his way into America's counter-espionage system. Or perhaps, he wondered, it was because the war had just started—this was in September, 1939—and the Consul was busy on more important matters.

But the Consul had not been twiddling his thumbs. He had flashed a secret report to Washington. State Department officials took it over to FBI headquarters at the Department of Justice.

Director Hoover's spy-fighters studied it carefully. They saw at once that this might be the chance they had been waiting for. They knew that the Nazis were busily building up espionage in this country. They even had a goodly number of suspects on their list. But what they needed was the kind of evidence that could be supplied by a man inside the spy-ring—somebody with intelligence and daring.

They decided it would be worth while to look over this man Sebold. If he were a phony or a double-crosser, he could be trapped easily enough.

When Sebold returned to the Consul for his letters, he heard words that made him smile happily. "Go back and write them a letter stating that you're accepting. Don't came back here any more. Contact will be made with you when you return to the United States."

He wrote the letter and quickly received orders to come to Hamburg. It wasn't easy for him to leave his kinfolk. But he knew, down in his heart, that he was doing right. He was helping to end the Nazi reign of terror over not just one family, but a world full of families. And something else gave him optimism. He knew that the Gestapo's chief weapon was terror. And if he refused to bow to it, there would be no purpose in the Gestapo's torturing his relatives.

In Hamburg, he was met by Gassner, whose rôle in the matter ended when he brought Sebold into Nikolaus' office. The spymaster was very well satisfied with himself. He believed he had another cowed man ready to go to work. Sebold was acting superbly.

Just enough eagerness for Nikolaus to be impressed with him, but not enough to make him suspicious. And in his arrogant Nazi conceit, the great Nikolaus—blinded by his firm belief that any man can be swayed by threat —decided that he had found the man he needed.

He stared at Sebold a few moments, then said, "You will not go to California. I have something else for you to do. You will be our paymaster in New York; you will distribute instructions and receive information. Do you think you can do it?"

Sebold leaned forward tensely. "If you teach me, I will gladly learn."

"Good! But perhaps your biggest job will be to set up and run a radio station. That, too, you will learn. You may perhaps wonder—why a radio station? It will be different later, I assure you, but right now, unfortunately, the damned British seem to control the Atlantic. That makes it dangerous for our couriers traveling on ships. They will continue carrying information on American ships. But for secret instructions, and so forth, we will pass over the heads of those British ships by radio."

[23]

He pushed a button, and into the office came Captain Sorau, his assistant.

"You will take Herr Sebold to your training school. You know what to do with him. When he is ready to sail, bring him back to me."

Sebold ambled out at Sorau's heels. His heart was thumping fast, but his stolid face betrayed nothing. He had passed the test! There was no turning back now!

"By the way," Sorau was saying, "it's best that we should not be seen together on the street. There are British eyes—even here in Hamburg. Should anybody ever ask you who I am, I am Hugo Sebold, your uncle." He stopped and wrote on a piece of paper. "Here is the address of the rooming-house where you will stay. And here is the address of my building. There are several whom I am coaching. Each of you has a private room. I shall spend much time with you, Herr Sebold. Be there promptly tomorrow morning at eight."

A strange three months followed; sometimes, Sebold wondered if he were dreaming. But his "uncle" Sebold was real enough. And he knew that Gassner had been no dream; nor had the beady-eyed man whom he had been told to address as "Dr. Rankin"—but who, in reality, he had learned, was the shadowy spymaster Nikolaus—Adolf Fritz Ritter.

Sorau first put him to work learning the international wireless code, and then instructed him in how to operate a wireless receiver and transmitter.

Then they went to work on photography. Sebold learned how to take and develop his own pictures, and enlarge them. He was shown a tiny piece of film.

"What do you see on it?" Sorau demanded.

"Nothing—a tiny speck only. A dot."

"Exactly. But there is something after all. We will now place it in an enlarger."

Sebold's eyes opened wide. What had looked like a dot on the film was now enlarged—and turned out to be a 50-word message.

Then he was instructed in the art of using a micro-camera—which would convert a full-size page of written instructions into a "micro."

"All this you will have to do yourself when you reach New York—so better pay close attention," Sorau said.

Finally, the day—late in January, 1940—came when the spy coach was satisfied that Sebold had mastered all necessary technique.

"Now for one final thing," he said. "The code. At last we have one those damned British can't crack. Here is a book you may have."

He handed to Sebold the best-seller, "All This and Heaven Too," by Rachel Field.

"Is it for me to read on the ship?" Sebold asked.

Sorau smiled. "Read it all you like. But hold on to it. It looks so innocent, doesn't it? A returning tourist carrying a nice American novel. Well then, suppose you get a message from us which consists of nothing but numbers. Here's what you do."

The first thing was to turn to a certain page in the book. Sorau pointed at the calendar, and said, "Today is January 24th." He proceeded to take the month of the year, the date of the month, add them together, and than add 20 more. It was the first month of the year, which gave the number 1. If it had been July, the number would have been 7. To the 1, Sorau added the date of the month, 24. This gave a total of 25. Now he added 20 more. The total was 45.

"So you turn to page 45 of your book," he concluded.

The rest was a matter of picking out words and letters on that page, in order to translate the numbers of the code message into words and sentence. The numbers each referred to such and such a word in such and such a line of page 45 or else to letters in the top line of the printed page.

"It doesn't seem too hard," said Sebold. "I will practice up on it."

"Not hard at all," said the instructor. "Just tedious

—and fool-proof. Because even if anybody finds the message numbers on you, they won't know what do to with them. And if they guess it requires a book, they won't know what book, or what page. Yes, we are proud of it. But we really didn't invent it; we just made it more complicated. This code happens to be based on one invented by an American traitor named Benedict Arnold."

The only graduation diploma Sebold got was a steamship ticket—he was due to leave Hamburg on the night of January 27th, and catch the S.S. *Washington,* bound for New York, at Genoa, Italy. He would go to Genoa by train. Since the *Washington* was an American liner, and he was an American citizen, he'd be safe from search by the British.

On that day, he was brought in to see Nikolaus again.

"I hear that you are now ready," said the spymaster. "From now on, your name will be Harry Sawyer. I am giving you $1,000. With half of it, you will buy necessary photographic equipment and radio equipment. Complete instructions will be given you before you leave. The other half you will pay to one of our agents. More money will be sent you from time to time, through a Mexican bank which will transfer it to your account in the Chase National Bank at New York. In New York, you will set up an office, and call it, 'The Diesel Research Company.' For erecting the radio station, you will receive further instructions from our man Siegler."

Sorau came in with five tiny cellophane envelopes, each containing a micro, and handed them to Sebold.

"Three of these micros," Nikolaus said, "contain all of your instructions, names and addresses, and so forth. Among them are the names and addresses and the passwords you should use, in contacting two agents to whom the other two micros should be delivered."

Sebold nodded.

Nikolaus stared at him a moment. "By the way, have you ever seen the Norden factory—where they make the bombsight?"

"No," Sebold replied. Then he added, "But I have heard of the famous bombsight. Maybe I can get hold of it—and make you a present of it."

Nikolaus smiled and winked at Sorau, then said to Sebold, "Don't worry about it—it's already in our possession."

This put something else in his mind, and he said, "There is one other person you are to see. He isn't mentioned in your micros. This is very important, and he is very important. Write down what I tell you, memorize it, and be sure to mail me back the slip of paper before you leave tonight, so that I can be sure you aren't carrying it with you."

He thought a moment, then said, "This is a personal message. You deliver it to Herman Lang, 5936 70th Avenue, Ridgewood, Long Island. You tell him to return by way of Japan and via Siberia to Germany, and all his expenses will be refunded, and we will give him a job. Approach him with these greetings: Rantzau, Berlin, Hamburg."

All three men arose, heiled Hitler, shook hands, and Sebold went to his rooming-house where he spent three hours drilling the Lang message into his brain. Then he mailed the slip to Nikolaus. Next, he took his watch apart and slipped the tiny micros into it. Then he packed.

Next he did what was only a normal thing for any American visitor to do—something that wouldn't arouse any Gestapo suspicions. He visited the American Consulate there in Hamburg. But in addition to attending to his passport visas, he left word to inform Washington that he was sailing and was due in New York on February 8th.

The trip across the Atlantic was an uneventful one. Once, Sebold couldn't resist the temptation, in the privacy of his stateroom, to open his watch and examine the micros carefully—but, of course, he could make nothing of them without an enlarger.

Shortly after the ship docked on the morning of February 8th, Sebold was secretly contacted by two men who identified themselves as an FBI Special Agent and a Department of State representative.

They hustled him into a taxi and sped up to Foley Square, to the skyscraper Federal Courthouse, at the top of which the FBI had its New York field headquarters.

Here, he met the Special-Agent-in-Charge. The latter gave him a warm greeting. "We've certainly been looking forward to seeing you. Hope you had a nice trip —and a sucessful one?"

Sebold smiled and said, "I think so."

Another man had come into the office—the Special Agent in charge of espionage investigations.

Sebold handed over the $1,000 and took the micros out of his watch.

"The money and these were given to me by the Gestapo," he explained. "The micros contain instructions to other spies and further instructions for myself to erect a radio station which should be in communication with Hamburg. I have also brought a memorized message for another spy, which I will now write down."

He wrote the Lang message and handed it over.

The FBI men were looking at him in astonishment. They had expected a man assigned to be a spy in an aircraft plant—but hardly a man assigned to handle details for the entire spy ring. This was the perfect chance for the kind of complete roundup Director Hoover wanted— if Sebold was genuine. It seemed almost too good to be true.

One Agent went off to the laboratory immediately to have the micros enlarged and translated. Another took Sebold away to question him about the Nazi spy setup.

Sebold was kept there that night. The FBI wanted to take no chance of anything happening to him.

The next day, he was called in to be present to see the micro enlargements. They turned out to contain a mine of evidence. One was to a Frederick Duquesne, asking him to begin collecting information on the American armed forces and instructing him to turn data over to Harry Sawyer.

"Sawyer is me," Sebold explained. "That's the name I was told to use."

Another micro was for an Everett Minster Roeder and a third was for a Lilly Stein, telling them also to work with "Sawyer," to whom they were to supply information.

The two micros for Sebold contained a wealth of leads. They gave the addresses of Duquesne, Roeder and Stein, and told what passwords Sebold should use in contacting them. They told him that Roeder was to receive $500 from Sebold. They revealed how to contact Irwin Wilhelm Siegler, who was to help Sebold with the radio station. And they gave full details about this secret station— where it should be located, the wattage it should use, what its frequency should be, etc.

While G-men went out to check on some of the leads, Sebold sat down to dictate a long statement covering everything he had seen, heard and done in Germany.

When the reports had finished coming in, the Special-Agent-in-Charge asked his chief assistant eagerly, "How does it look?"

"Perfectly swell! I'm convinced that Sebold is the man we've been needing. There are several intensely interesting things in these reports. The man Duquesne turns out to be a spy and crook of forty years' standing, whom we've long suspected. The man Roeder, to whom $500 is to be paid, is an engineer and designer at the Sperry Gyroscope Company."

That wasn't all. Both men remembered some evidence in a previous Nazi spy case—testimony that a courier from Germany had brought two $1,000 bills for somebody working in a gyroscope company. The FBI had been unable to discover the identity of this high-priced German hireling. Now arose the suspicion: Was it Roeder?"

And there was something more. Investigation of Herman Lang showed that he was an inspector at the Carl

L. Norden Company—manufacturers of the precious, secret Norden bombsight. He had gone to Germany in 1938. Could this mean that the bombsight's secret was in German hands?

If so, the only reason why Lang was being asked to come back to Germany now by the Gestapo was to give information on any improvements that had been made on the bombsight.

A full report went to FBI Director Hoover. And his instructions came back in a few, forceful words. There must be the utmost secrecy. There should be no arrests —yet. The Gestapo should be tricked into revealing its activities further.

Five

THE FBI DECIDED to edit and control all information going to Hamburg, so that the Gestapo would learn nothing harmful to America. And, when the investigation had served its purpose, there should be a lightning roundup of all members of the ring.

Director Hoover came to New York frequently after that to keep an eye on progress in the case and to divert it at crucial phases.

Meanwhile, Sebold was being given instructions in how he was to maintain secret contact with the FBI, and what he was to do. In view of the fact that he had no other chance to earn a living, because he was now working for the Government, he was given a salary of $50 a week. Any money he received for himself from Germany was to be kept until the end of the case when it would go to the American government.

As for the radio station he was to erect, and other equipment—he didn't have to worry. The FBI was only too glad to give him anything he needed.

He immediately complied with Hamburg instructions and sent a cable to his "Uncle Hugo," informing Sorau that all was well.

Arrived safe. Had pleasant trip.

Bill.

Also in line with instructions, he took a room at the Y. M. C. A., at 5 West 63rd Street, in Manhattan. The FBI rented an office for him in a building at 152 West 42nd Street—only a few feet away from bustling Times Square. It was a tiny office, with an even tinier little workroom where he could develop film and do other technical work.

He shopped around for a magnifying glass with which to read micros, and bought a reduction camera similar to the one he had used in Hamburg when learning how to make a micro.

Now everything seemed to be all set for the big fellow to demonstrate what he could do in the rôle of counter-spy. Needless to say, the FBI was watching him closely to make absolutely sure he wasn't up to trickery on behalf of the Gestapo—but it wasn't long before he demonstrated that he was worthy of the trust placed in him.

For this one man who enlisted on the side of Uncle Sam, there were half a dozen who set about to betray America.

One of Nikolaus' new recruits was Hartwig Richard Kleiss, who was chief cook on the U. S. Lines S. S. *America,* and later on the same lines' luxury liners, *President Harding* and *Manhattan.* Originally, he was a native of Germany. He bragged often of how, in the first World War, he served on a German sea raider that sank seventeen Allied ships.

The raider had to run into Newport News, Virginia, for repairs in 1915, and her entire crew was interned under rules of war. When America entered the war, Kleiss went to a Georgia prison camp. After the war, he decided to earn American dollars instead of going back to starving Germany.

In 1931, he became an American citizen. Five years later, he showed where his sympathies really lay, by moving his wife and sixteen-year-old daughter to Germany.

In that same year, he got into trouble with Hamburg Customs officials who caught him trying to smuggle money out of Germany. He was grilled by the Gestapo. To clear himself, he wrote a long letter to the head of the Customs at Hamburg, in which he boasted of his love for Germany and of how he had staffed his ship's kitchen with Germans only.

He said he had turned American citizen solely in order to keep his job with the American steamship line:

After a hard inner struggle, I was compelled to remain where my income was, and naturally I surrendered, against my inner desire, my German citizenship . . . but I have regarded it as my duty to have my foreign income taxed in Germany . . .

It was always my effort to recruit the ninety employees under me only from German kitchens. Almost without exception, they were natives of Hamburg. . . . As a German, I have never hesitated to get monthly supplies in Hamburg to the amount of 25,000 marks. I could have secured supplies just as cheap or cheaper in foreign ports, and this is perhaps the only sharp practice with which I willingly burden by conscience. The *Manhattan*, flagship of the U. S. Lines, stops at Hamburg thirteen times a year, and other American liners follow her example. As a result, I can say with satisfaction that I have supplied Hamburg's economic life with at least one-third of a million marks.

He paid a fine and was let go. But the Gestapo remembered. Its files had a long memory. And when Nikolaus needed new spies and couriers late in 1939, after the war broke out, Kleiss' name was put on the prospect list.

When the *Manhattan* made a stop at Genoa, Italy, her head chef found a Gestapo emissary waiting for him on the dock.

"It has been decided, Herr Kleiss," he said, "that it is time for you to do something for Germany." He explained.

Kleiss protested that spying was too dangerous.

"But not as dangerous as a concentration camp would be," the other said. "As you know very well, you cannot escape us. And that 1936 smuggling affair makes us doubt your loyalty. This is your chance to redeem yourself."

And the sweating chief cook agreed to begin hiding American military secrets among his pots and pans.

Others came into the ring more willingly. One was Franz Joseph Stigler who was also working on American ships only in order to get enough maney to live in comparative luxury in Germany. He had been head baker on the *America* and was now on the *Manhattan* with

Kleiss. They made a hard-working spy pair—Kleiss who sent his secret messages under the name of "Jimmy Hard," and Stigler, whose spy alias was "Aufzug," a German word meaning "organized."

But not all of them were followers of the sea.

There was Carl Alfred Reuper, whose American citizenship papers didn't mean as much to him as his membership in the Chicago branch of the German-American Bund. He had been too young to serve in the Kaiser's World War army, but had joined the Reichswehr in 1922, and served six years until he was discharged because he wasn't considered quite right in the head.

He came to America, went to work as a machinist in Chicago, got married and took out citizenship papers. But life wasn't complete until he joined the Bund and could heil Hitler to his heart's content.

In April, 1939, he took his wife to Germany to show her what Utopia really looked like. After a while, their money ran out and they didn't have enough to return to America.

The Gestapo had been watching him, as it watched every other visitor from America. One day, one of its agents came to Reuper.

"We have heard about your financial distress," he said. "And we will be glad to help."

In return, Reuper was to worm his way into some airplane factory in America, and send Hamburg reports on production and new plane secrets.

The machinist heiled Hitler and said he certainly would do it. Then he went into a long speech—down with America and up with the Third Reich.

"You sound very convincing," said the Gestapo man. "There is something else we will have you do. You're to talk with the workers over there—make them dissatisfied, get them to strike, promote discord and bad feeling. It's absolutely necessary to paralyze American airplane production. Too many planes are already going to England."

Reuper was taught how to make photostats of anything he came across that looked interesting. And he was instructed to communicate with Hamburg by secret-ink letters.

He watched, with mouth wide open, as his instructor scrawled something with a pen on paper—and there was no writing visible—then the instructor touched the sheet with a drop of fluid, and the writing appeared in blue.

He was given a bottle of the fluid. "You'll get more when you need it."

He was told he would be a "lone wolf" in America, and he swelled with importance, not realizing that the Gestapo figured he wasn't too reliable—his loud-mouthed Nazi talk might get him into trouble. The Gestapo didn't want him to become acquainted with other spies, who might be involved if he got caught.

"But it will be necessary that you know at least one colleague," he was told. So, just before Reuper sailed in January, 1940, he was introduced to a man with a thin, high-boned face, jutting chin and pig eyes—Axel Wheeler-Hill.

"Herr Wheeler-Hill is still studying radio with us," the Gestapo man said. "But when he returns to America, we want you to see each other and work together at times."

Reuper shook the other pupil's hand eagerly. "Are you related," he asked, "to James Wheeler-Hill, secretary of the German-American Bund?"

"I should say I am! He's my brother."

Six

DESPITE THESE NEW recruits, Nikolaus knew there was something lacking. He could threaten men into becoming spies, he could hire human scum, he could use Nazi crackpots—but what he needed most were a few intelligent man in important American defense posts, men who would serve Hitler out of devotion to the "cause."

It seemed that such men were almost impossible to get. And Nikolaus, in his Nazi arrogance, couldn't understand why. He couldn't understand that any intelligent, decent American of German descent wanted nothing to do with Hitler or his gangsters.

But Nikolaus kept trying.

German-born Albert A. Vollmecke was very well satisfied with his adopted country, the United States. He lived happily with his wife in Washington, D. C. He had come to America in 1927, been naturalized in 1933, and in 1934, joined the Civil Aeronautics Authority. By 1938, he had become chief of its engineering section.

Inasmuch as every airport the CAA built fitted into Uncle Sam's defense picture, Vollmecke's importance to the Nazis can easily be seen.

Once or twice every year, for several years, he had exchanged letters with a boyhood chum who had stayed in Germany, Wilhelm Loehr. They had grown up together in the same town of Braunschweig. Vollmecke had gone into engineering. Loehr had served with the Kaiser's air force. Then Loehr had gone into furniture manufacturing and Vollmecke had come to America.

When the Nazis built up their *Luftwaffe,* "Air force," Loehr had gone back, as a factory test pilot. And from the questionnaire he had to fill out for the Gestapo, Nikolaus learned of his friendship with Vollmecke. Loehr was put to work.

Shortly before Christmas, 1938, Vollmecke got a letter from him. In addition to the usual seasonal greetings, it said, "By the way, Albert, I have a very good friend named Eilers who lives in New York, and makes monthly trips to Germany. I would personally appreciate it if you would drop in and see him when you are next in New York City." The letter gave Eilers' address.

Loehr very carefully didn't mention that he was back in the German *Luftwaffe*. So far as Vollmecke knew, his friend was still in the furniture business. Therefore, it wasn't caution that guided him. He was simply too busy—and he forgot the matter.

But the Gestapo didn't forget.

The man "Eilers" was Heinrich Carl Eilers, a partly bald, big-nosed library steward aboard that spy-teeming American liner, *Manhattan*.

His wife, Gertrude, was a Munich cabaret dancer who was in reality a Gestapo informer; she turned in boy friends who showed any traces of disloyalty to Hitler.

In December, 1939, a year after Loehr first asked Vollmecke to look up Eilers, the library steward got Gestapo orders to leave his ship the next time it touched an Italian port, long enough for him to make a quick visit to Loehr in Germany.

Eilers obeyed. "It is absolutely necessary for you," Loehr instructed him, "to find out whether Vollmecke will work for us. You will have to go to Washington, D. C., because I haven't heard a word from him. A letter of introduction will be supplied."

Then he went on to outline Vollmecke's importance, and what information the steward should seek from the CAA official.

Eilers heard nothing more about it until three months later, when the *Manhattan* stopped at Genoa, Italy. There he was visited by the spy ring's Genoa agent, Carlos Pitzuck, who handed him a letter to be given to Vollmecke.

One afternoon in March, 1940, the CAA official returned to his apartment house from his office and found a letter in his mail slot. It was on stationery of the S. S. *Manhattan*. He read:

[37]

Dear Mr. Vollmecke: My friend Wilhelm Loehr asked me to look you up. As I did not meet anybody home, I will be back around six o'clock—Heinrich Eilers.

Early evening brought Eilers. He entered Vollmecke's apartment only after looking around to see that he wasn't being followed.

"Are you Herr Vollmecke?" he asked in German.

"Yes," the other said. "But I prefer to speak in English."

Eilers looked at him carefully. He saw a short, impeccably dressed man with an intelligent face. Vollmecke spoke good English, but with traces of a German accent.

"I have brought this to you from Loehr," Eilers said, and handed over an envelope.

Vollmecke tore it open and found a Christmas card inside. It contained greetings from Loehr and some writing:

Dear Albert and Maja (Vollmecke's wife): I've not heard from you in a long time. My friend Eilers brings you greetings from the Homeland. Here, the same situation is arising which we faced in the other war. But we stand better technically. The *Luftwaffe* is powerful. The men who served with me in the other war are to-day great men. . . . (He went on to mention several names of German fliers and engineers) . . . When my friend Eilers calls, you may trust him. I have known him many years. He is married to a Munich girl. . . .

"I don't understand," Vollmecke said. "What does he mean to trust you? What is he doing these days, anyway?"

"I thought you knew," Eilers said. "He's an important test pilot for the Luftwaffe. I see him regularly. And I am to bring to him whatever you can tell us about American aviation."

Vollmecke gritted his teeth. So he was being asked to be a spy?

Eilers left him in no doubt about it. He came closer to Vollmecke and pulled some New York newspaper clippings from his pocket. They dealt with American war-plane deliveries to England and France.

"This is the sort of thing Loehr is interested in," he explained. "Except that, from you, it would be accurate and complete. Tell me, are your duties strictly commercial, how much do they deal with military aviation?"

Vollmecke stood up, went to the door and opened it. "If Loehr is interested in such things, he had better address his inquiries through official channels in Washington. Good-bye, Mr. Eilers."

The spy courier smiled. "Perhaps you do not trust me. But you will. Whenever you have any information to send, which you don't want to risk being caught in the mails by British censorship, I will be more than glad to take it along."

It wasn't long before Vollmecke had turned the entire matter over to the FBI.

Three months later, the Nazis tried again. Vollmecke received a postcard from Eilers. It contained a message written in guarded language:

I am sending you some magazines under separate cover which will interest you. Meanwhile, if you have anything for Wilhelm, I will be more than glad to take it along.

Vollmecke's evidence joined the rest being amassed by the spy-fighters of the FBI.

For Director Hoover's men had lost no time using William Sebold as their ace-in-the-hole. Ten days after his arrival in New York, he had been coached thoroughly, set up in his office near Times Square and told to begin posing as "Harry Sawyer," Gestapo emissary to Nazi spies in New York City.

Following the instructions he had received from the Nazis, he went out to deliver the micro to Lilly Stein; it had, of course, already been copied at the FBI laboratory.

She lived in a ground-floor apartment at 127 East 54th

Street. Sebold rang the buzzer, and the door was opened by the beauteous artist's model herself. She was in a clinging negligee. It was eight o'clock at night, and she was preparing to dress for a party.

Big Sebold stared a moment, then stolidly uttered the password:

"I bring you greetings from Bachenal and Grinsing."

Lilly nodded, "Yes—I was notified. Come in."

He handed her the tiny film and said, "I will go now. The micro will explain everything. I will return to pick up anything you will have to give me."

He ambled out, and reported to Agent Donegan, who was directing him, that everything seemed to have gone well on this, the first contact with a member of the spy ring.

His next step was to deliver the micro of instructions to the professional spy, Duquesne, the film which gave that cunning plotter eighteen formidable assignments.

Here too, Sebold and his FBI colleagues knew in advance what was in the micro. And they knew that Duquesne must be a master spy indeed if he could fulfil all of the Nazi requests. Here were some of them:

Duquesne was to find out whether the American Telephone and Telegraph Company had invented a secret "bombing ray," and if so, he was to steal the secret. The ray was supposed to guide a bomber to an objective; and when the bomber was over the target, a second ray released the bombs. Other assignments were:

Find out all you can about Professor Bullard, of Hobart College, the chemical warfare expert, and the Army uniform that will stop mustard gas which he is supposed to have perfected.

Is there being manufactured in the United States an anti-aircraft shell with an electric eye? What is the shell's caliber? How does the complicated, delicate mechanism in the shell stand up to firing shock? How does this shell compare in accuracy with the ordinary shell?

Provide all new developments in bacteriological warfare—the spreading of disease germs—from airplanes.

What are the new developments in American Army gasmasks?

How about the new trench-crusher? We hear that the United States has developed such a mysterious machine which will ride over trenches and destroy them. Furnish the names of the manufacturers, the size of deliveries, and for whom they are being made.

What are the new developments in the gun turret design for Sunderland flying boats which Captain Lungstedt is working on?

Find out if there are going to Europe any single warplanes, or squadrons, with personnel of the U. S. Army and Navy camouflaged as volunteer troops. Report immediately when there are any signs of war mobilization in America.

We have read in a magazine about a metal-cleaning fluid developed by the Curaz Company, Malden, Mass. Get some of it for us.

That's how the instructions went. Germany wanted to know about a new American "anti-fog device" and about the Sperry range-finder. Germany, quite willing to use germ warfare, was nervously wondering if America was preparing anything like that too. Many of the assignments were simply shots in the dark—a fear of American surprise weapons. And it was Duquesne's job to provide the answers.

In addition, he had a general assignment which was as important as any other, and probably more so. It was to report on the airplane production and airplane motor output by our leading manufacturers.

Germany wanted to know, it was obvious, how far she dared go in defying American might. The micro contained a long list of names and plane and motor manufacturers he should investigate: Curtiss, North American, Glenn Martin, Douglas, Boeing, Pratt & Whitney, Lockheed (except that the Nazis got twisted in spelling the last and wrote it, "Lougheed")

So Sebold carried out the orders in his own micros and
wrote a letter to 'Colonel Frederick Joubert Duquesne,"
at a Wall Street address:

My dear Colonel: I have arrived from Hamburg where
Nikolaus and George informed me that you too are a
patent attorney interested in matters similar to mine.
I would like to know where and when it would be pos-
sible to meet you. Believe me to be most sincerely—
Harry Sawyer.

He received a telephone call from Duquesne asking
him to come to his office on the 31st floor of the Wall
Street office building.

But Duquesne didn't have a private office, he merely
shared office facilities with a half-dozen other men, all of
them being small-time stock brokers. He was using the
Wall Street address for "front," and posing as a stock
broker himself, engaged in selling R.K.O. stock .

Sebold walked in stolidly and asked for Duquesne.
The spy came up and said warmly, "Hello, Harry. Take
a chair."

But two of the other men had sidled up; they were
going to see if they could steal Duquesne's "stock cus-
tomer." Duquesne went to a desk and scribbled something on a pink slip, which he dropped in Sebold's hand.
It read:

We will go out. Cannot talk here.

So they went down to a near-by Automat. Here,
Sebold slipped across the micro, which Duquesne
dropped in his pocket. Continuing to follow his instructions, Sebold began describing himself as a Diesel expert
who had done much work with the Siemens-Schuckert
Company, the German counterpart of our General Electric Company.

Duquesne nodded. "I, too, work with them. They are
interested in my invention of a floating dock."

They chatted on about inventions. Sebold had seen

[42]

from the first, when he gazed into those cunning eyes, that here would be no easy man to outwit. The FBI had warned him not to expect too much from a first meeting with any of the spies. But Duquesne was more than taciturn; he was suspicious.

"You don't speak English badly," he said. "How'd you learn it?"

"Oh, I was here once before. But I didn't make out very good—sold silk stockings from door to door, and like that."

They finally parted, Sebold saying he would contact Duquesne again in a week or so.

When he called again, Duquesne led the way to an Automat. Then he walked with Sebold over to City Hall Park, where they sat on a bench.

"We call this LaGuardia's Ranch," he sneered.

But after an hour's conversation, Sebold had nothing but vague talk about inventions.

This didn't worry the FBI too much. They expected that Duquesne would cautiously contact Hamburg first to make sure that Sebold was trustworthy.

Sebold also made a return visit to Lilly Stein. Here, too, he got no information, but for a different reason. Lilly claimed that she had nothing to give him.

"But one of our men in Detroit may send something soon," she promised.

Sebold had to be satisfied with that. There was another Gestapo order he had to obey—to deliver Nikolaus' personal message to the man Herman Lang, whom the FBI now strongly suspected of having sold the Norden bomb-sight secret to Germany.

At first, Sebold wondered if the man had flown. Because when the counter-spy went to the Ridgewood, Long Island, address he had memorized, he found nobody living in the apartment house by the name of Lang.

But finally, after scouring around, he located a janitor who gave him Lang's new address. It was 74-36 64th Place, Glendale, Queens.

[43]

At noon on March 23rd, Sebold trudged up the stairs at that address and rang the bell.

A snub-nosed, sad-faced man opened the door.

"Are you Mr. Lang?"

"Yes—come in."

Sebold took a chair and opened up with, "I have just come from Germany where I met an old friend of yours."

Instead of answering, Lang began walking around, throwing covert glances at his visitor, until finally Sebold wondered if he had the right man and inquired, "Are you Herman Lang—who was in Germany in 1938 for a visit?"

"Yes, I was in Germany in 1938," the other answered cautiously.

"Well then, here is what I was instructed to tell you."

He gave Lang the message from Nikolaus ordering him to return to Germany by way of Japan and the Trans-Siberian Railroad—into Germany; Lang's expenses would be refunded and he would be given something to do. There were also the regards from "Rantzau."

But Lang fairly exuded suspicion. "I have no desire to go to Germany. I am an American citizen."

"So am I," Sebold replied. "And I'm something else."

Lang digested that hint a moment. "Where are your credentials?"

Sebold laughed. "Isn't it enough that I know Rantzau and Sorau and the rest?" Lang still stared. So Sebold took a chance of being arrested as a spy—if Lang were innocent of espionage himself.

"I'm here for one thing," Sebold said. "To deliver a message to you, and to transmit information. I'm with the German espionage."

Lang lit a cigarette nervously, then said gutturally, "I want nothing to do with you. I don't trust you."

Sebold arose and said coolly, "As you wish. I shall see you again one of these days."

As soon as he stepped into the hallway, the door slammed behind him.

But that visit was far from a failure. As days passed, and there came no complaint or tip-off from Lang to the FBI or to the Norden Company that he had been approached by a Nazi spy, it became pretty clear that he was far from an innocent man himself.

The FBI could afford to wait. It expected that sooner or later Lang would open up to Sebold.

Seven

THE FOURTH SPY Sebold contacted turned out to be easier than the rest. He was Everett Roeder, the engineer and designer at the Sperry Gyroscope Company.

Unlike most of the others, Roeder was American-born, but of German descent. He greedily accepted the $500 which Sebold had brought from Hamburg. But he declined to give any more information.

"Not until I get some more pay," he said. "This is a business proposition with me."

So Sebold promised to inform Hamburg that more money was needed.

Roeder was a pudgy little technician who wore thick-lensed spectacles. He was quite unsuspicious — the money had convinced him.

"So you're a new man here?" he said. "Do you know George Sessler?—He's a ship's steward who used to contact me."

Sebold shook his head, but made a mental note to inform the FBI about this Sessler. Unfortunately, the FBI found that the man had gone back to Germany to stay.

But Roeder was placed under surveillance. He would hardly have been suspected, had it not been for Sebold. He was one of the most respected citizens of Merrick, Long Island. He possessed both state and town permits for the possession of gunpowder and a cartridge-filling machine, because he belonged to several rifle clubs and to the National Rifle Association. Among other weapons, he owned six pistols, nine rifles, and several shotguns. He was one of the few really "respectable" members of the spy ring.

In order to inform Hamburg that he had complied with instructions and to relay Roeder's request for more money, Sebold had to use the courier, Irwin Wilhelm Siegler.

He had been chief butcher on the S. S. *America* and

was now a butcher on the spy ship *Manhattan*. He had come to Sebold's office and introduced himself as a courier, explaining that he would carry most of Sebold's communications until the radio station was built.

"But your ship doesn't go to Germany," Sebold pumped him. "How will you deliver my messages?"

"Through letter-boxes on our ports-of-call. We've Duarte in Lisbon, Pitzuck in Genoa, and so on."

Later, Siegler confided that he had served a prison term in Germany for trying to smuggle money. He had been freed when he agreed to turn spy courier.

"Strangely enough," he said, "my partner in that money scheme, Erich Strunck, also made the same bargain to get out of jail. He's now a waiter on the Export Liner *Siboney* and one of our best men. You'll meet him soon."

Siegler turned out to be more than a courier. He was a contact man who introduced spies to each other. Through him, Sebold met such other couriers aboard the *Manhattan* as Kleiss, the chief cook, and Stigler, the baker.

Siegler and Stigler gave Sebold some trouble for a time, because of the similarity in their names—until he began referring to them, in his reports to the FBI, by the aliases they used in spy work. Stigler was known as "Aufzug" and Siegler as "Metzger," the German word for "butcher."

Within a few days, thanks to Metzger, Sebold met some more of the spy ring's couriers. They seemed to infest the Atlantic. One of them, Paul Fehse, was a cook aboard the *Manhattan*. The big ape-faced Adolph Walischewski was a steward aboard the S. S. *Uruguay* of the Moore-McCormack Line. Conradin Dold was a chief steward who changed around between the *Excalibur*, *Excambion* and *Siboney* of the American Export Line.

As a result, the FBI kept increasing the number of Special Agents necessary to watch all these intriguers, see where they went when ashore, whom they met, and note whenever they carried suspicious-looking packages.

But there were even couriers by air. One day, Aufzug gave Sebold a telephone number, and asked him to call it.

Sebold complied, and spoke with a man who said "This is Max. I have brought something for you. I will be at your office in an hour."

The man turned out to be Rene Emanuel Mezenen, a native of France but now an American citizen. He was a steward on the Pan-American Airways plane *Dixie Clipper,* flying between the United States and Lisbon, Portugal.

He handed Sebold a micro, explaining "It's from Dr. Dobler in Lisbon."

"I don't recognize the name, but I know of a Duarte there," said Sebold.

"It's the same man. You are to deliver the micro to Jimmy Dunn, but what it says for him to do applies, in general, to all the other agents."

Jimmie Dunn, Sebold had learned, meant Duquesne, so he prepared to see that wily individual again. But first, he turned the micro over to the FBI. Enlarged, it proved that the Nazis were already becoming intensely worried about American armed might, even though this was only April, 1940. The micro read in part:

In the future, technical questions do not interest us as much as military ones. Get us:

A—Exact strength of the U. S. A. Air Force, listing separately the number of men in flying and ground crews.

B—Details concerning location of flying schools for fliers, length of training, number of students.

C—Especially interested in all kinds of instruction books and manuals, particularly those not available on open market.

D—Of paramount importance, if pilots are being trained for England, where are they trained, how many, when and where expected to leave, by ship or air, what route expected to take, the days of their departure. These questions pertain to Canada as well as U. S. A. It may be necessary to find friends in air force itself. I am sending $500 for this purpose.

This made it clear that the Nazis, in addition to wanting to learn our air strength, wanted their sea raiders to know where and when to meet American pilots going over to fight for England.

Sebold looked up Duquesne again. This time, it was entirely different. The ace spy had evidently checked with Hamburg and was now satisfied.

He looked curiously at the micro. "I'll enlarge it tonight," he said. "Meanwhile, I've been doing some pretty hard work on those other assignments, and I've sent considerable stuff across. But how much do they expect a man can do with only $300 a month? They'd better raise the ante—and you can tell them so for me."

But when Sebold saw him a few days later, Duquesne was enthusiastic. "The micro says $500 is coming for me, to use in bribing American Army aviators. That shows that maybe Hamburg is loosening up a little with the purse strings. Let me know right away when the dough comes, will you Harry?"

"Sure," said "Harry Sawyer." Then he added, "Have you nothing for me yet?"

"No, I'm sending my stuff by mail. My girl friend mails it for me. I use one of our letter-boxes in China. The stuff I've sent so far isn't so important that there'd be any harm if the British intercepted it."

Meanwhile, the FBI was rushing with work on the radio station that Sebold was to use for communication with the Gestapo bosses. The sooner the station was in operation, the easier it would be for the FBI to sift nearly every bit of spy information being sent to Germany.

Not only that, but the Gestapo itself was showing signs of impatience. Metzger, on his last trip from Lisbon, had brought a note relayed from Hamburg which stated simply, "Have you put up the radio station yet?"

[49]

No, it wasn't up yet, but it was going up. And with the exception of a few important details, it was going up as the Gestapo had ordered.

The instructions to Sebold called for a secret short-wave station, receiver and transmitter, to be put up in some isolated spot on Long Island. But the FBI wasn't content to use any cheap, portable equipment. It wanted an outfit good enough to lick trans-Atlantic weather most of the time, because it was at least as eager as the Gestapo for communication to take place.

Hamburg had ordered that the secret station's call letters be "CQDXvW-2," and that it should transmit on a frequency band between 14,300 and 14,400 kilocycles. Sebold's code signature was to be "Seeb" and the person on the German end of the line would be "TH." The German station itself would be a secret one and would answer to the call letters of "DOR."

The code Sebold would use in sending and receiving messages would be the one already described, involving use of the best-seller novel, *All This and Heaven Too.*

The reason the Gestapo wanted Sebold's station to be a secret one was clear. The American Government requires a license for every radio transmitter. But a German spy, as Sebold was supposed to be, could hardly apply for such a license and thereby give his game away. What the Gestapo didn't seem to realize is that our Federal Communications Commission, in charge of radio, has a staff of "radio detectives" whose job it is to track down unlicensed and illegal stations.

The FBI didn't want the FCC to be getting any wrong ideas about Station CQDXvW-2, so it tipped off this sister outfit of the Government that the station was to be an undercover one operated for FBI purposes.

So far as the location of the station was concerned, the FBI obeyed the Gestapo's instructions, because the G-men themselves wanted the station to be secret.

Before long, they had chosen the place, a Long Island bungalow so hidden by hedges and flower bushes that it would have been a honeymooning couple's paradise.

As an added precaution against anybody who might have rented the house in the past, the FBI men changed all locks in the house.

There were some other FBI touches that Nikolaus back in Hamburg wouldn't have cared so much for.

For one thing, all incoming messages were to be recorded on wax discs, to be used as incontrovertible evidence when the case came to trial, and also to be sure that nothing could be lost in the message.

Another thing, Sebold was not to be the station's operator. He had been trained for this task at the Hamburg spy school, but the FBI had a different idea. It figured that he would have plenty to do contacting members of the gang.

Two such men were chosen. One was a curly-haired young Special Agent who had joined the FBI six years before. He was one of Director Hoover's specialists, a licensed Class A radio operator. He would do the sending and receiving.

The other was a Special Agent who had become Sebold's main adviser and contact with the FBI. He was assigned to coach Sebold in the latter's contact with the spies and to help code and decode messages.

As the station neared readiness, Sebold sent a courier message to Hamburg, informing his "Uncle Hugo" that he would be ready to go on the air by May 15th.

His reply came in the form of a telephone call from the courier Metzger, who said, "I've just come in on the *Manhattan.* I've brought something for you from Lisbon. It was relayed there from Hamburg. I'll meet you in an hour at the Black Eagle Café, on 11th Avenue near 21st Street."

When Sebold got there, Metzger thrust a brown envelope into his hand, explaining, "It's a micro inside."

The FBI enlarged the tiny film and read these last-minute orders:

[51]

Dear Friend—I gathered from your explanation that you probably will be ready for operations on May 15. Beginning on the appointed day, call for 14 days at 6 o'clock Eastern Standard Time, every 10 minutes calling CQDXvW-2. We will recognize you in that you will give the small letter "v." We will look for you between 14,300 and 14,000. For our call letter use AOR instead of DOR and keep it up until 7 o'clock at 10-minute intervals.

A great deal will depend on atmospheric conditions. Don't become impatient if it shouldn't work for days.

There still remained a couple of weeks of adjusting to be done on the Long Island station and the FBI men pushed ahead eagerly on the task.

Eight

M EANWHILE, UNKNOWN to Sebold and the FBI, a sort of competitor arrived on the scene. He was wolf-faced Axel Wheeler-Hill who stepped off the liner *Manhattan* in New York with $500 of Gestapo money in his pocket and orders to set up a secret short-wave tie-up with Germany. But his job was different from Sebold's. Wheeler-Hill was assigned to concentrate on freight ships. He and those helping him were to prowl around the waterfronts, spying on the munitions being loaded for Britain. Then he was to radio Germany, so that Nazi U-boats could sink the vessels.

The Gestapo had made no mistake in choosing Wheeler-Hill. He was a Nazi fanatic, and a member of a thoroughly Nazi family. He was a naturalized American, but that made no difference to him. Axel was longing for the day when the United States would be a Nazi province, and he would be a Nazi bigshot.

In other words he detested working for an honest living. He had been born a "Baltic German" in Libau, Latvia. He had attended a cadet school in Russia, and then had fought against the Bolsheviks in the Russian Revolution.

In 1923, he came to America, shortly after the arrival of his elder brother, James. Axel worked on an ice wagon for a while. From 1929 to 1938, he ran a trolley car in New York City for the Third Avenue Railway Company.

In those years, his sly brother James had become secretary of the Nazi front organization in America, the German-American Bund. And Axel attended Bund meetings and heiled Hitler with the rest of them.

But the Nazi revolution in America was so slow in coming that Axel got disgusted. In 1938, he took his wife and three children and returned to Germany. For a while, he worked in a machine factory in southern Germany as a timekeeper.

But the wages were low and Axel wished he had

stayed in America where he could live more comfortably while working for the Nazi cause. And then, in September, 1939, the war broke out; the factory turned to the manufacture of munitions and Axel was out of his job.

Down at the heels, he looked up another of his brothers, Kurt, who was a small-time German Government official. Kurt said he'd look around. A few days later, he summoned Axel.

"I've the solution for you. How would you like to go back to America as one of our agents? There'll be good pay, you know what our plans are regarding America. You'll be sitting pretty when we come over there."

"Sure," said Axel. "What am I supposed to do?"

"Here's sixty marks. Go to Hamburg. A man, Frederick Schroeder, will meet you at the train depot. He's from the secret service, and will tell you all about it."

Schroeder turned out to be a tall, thin man, who quickly bundled Axel into a taxi and drove him out to a bungalow at the edge of the city.

"British agents are becoming more and more troublesome," he explained. "We don't want them to learn whom we're sending to America."

They went to a room and Schroeder outlined the proposition.

"We are glad to hear that you want to return to America. We will pay your fare, and will take care of your family—they will remain here. Your job will be to get trustworthy helpers. With them you are to watch the docks all around New York, Hoboken and Brooklyn. You are to observe the ships on which warplanes and other munitions are being loaded for England and France. Pay attention not only to armed British freighters but also to neutral ships, whether they be Dutch, Polish, Swedish and what-not. Understand?"

Axel nodded.

"Then you are to flash us the word. Our submarines will do the rest. All you have to do is tell us what ship, and when she sails."

Schroeder went on to explain, "You will be trained in the use of secret short-wave radio with which to inform us. We have other agents there in America, but you will work with your own men. We don't want to take the chance of one weakling betraying the rest."

Soon afterward, Axel was studying hard at the Hamburg spy school. A German Army corporal gave him a smattering of the international wireless code and the fundamentals of operating a radio transmitter. Another tutor instructed him in the use of code.

It was the same system as that taught to Sebold, the use of words contained in a best-seller. The only difference was in the book Axel was to use. It was David Hume's lurid tale, *Half-Way to Horror*.

As I have related already, Axel was introduced one day to Carl Reuper, who was returning to America to spy in aircraft plants and cause as much labor trouble as he could. The men were told to be of assistance to each other in America.

By March, 1940, Axel was still pretty much of an amateur in running a wireless transmitter. But he was told to sail immediately for New York. Just as Germany was sending raw crews into submarines in her desperate attempt to knock out England before America could build up her war machine, she was sending out raw spies. The need was urgent.

"You can learn the rest about radio at some school in New York," he was told. "In the meantime, you will begin at once to watch activities on the waterfront. Whatever you learn should be airmailed at once to this address: S. T. Neeland, Schaumburgstrasse, Bremen. Or else you should deliver it to a ship courier who will call on you."

He was given a train-and-steamer ticket, and $500. "You are to look up Reuper at once when you reach New York. He is to get $100. The rest you will use in buying equipment and setting up your station. Reuper will help you."

And so another spy came to America along the favorite spy route, by train to Genoa, and by an American steamer from that Italian port to New York, an innocent-looking tourist carrying a copy of the popular book with the rather significant title, *Half-Way to Horror*.

Two days later, he called the telephone number Reuper had given him back in Hamburg.

Reuper arranged for a meeting in front of the information booth at the Pennsylvania Railroad Station, at 2 P. M.

They went to a tavern for a few drinks. Axel handed over the $100, which Reuper took greedily. "I get money now and then through a Swiss bank," he said. "But it's little enough for the work I do."

He went on to boast of what he had been doing. First, he had spent several weeks looking for the kind of a job he had been ordered to take. At last he had found it, as a machinist with Air Associates, Inc. Reuper's job was in the experimental section.

"You can well imagine," he boasted, "what valuable information I am able to pick up, and the kind of blueprints I take home to copy."

"How do you get them over to the other side?"

"By ship couriers. One of them is Walischewski, a steward on the *Washington*. But I had to get rough with him a couple of days ago. The big boob—why he has two grown sons fighting for the *Fuehrer*. And yet he turns sissy on me. He warns me about a new American law forbidding any seamen to carry private packages or messages. As if we give a damn about any American law!"

Then Axel spoke of his own problems.

"What you'd better do is get a job of some kind," Reuper advised. "Hamburg doesn't seem to remember that we've got to live."

So Axel got a job in a soft-drink bottling company. On the side, he enrolled at a Y. M. C. A. for a course in radio.

Reuper continued to be helpful. When he saw that

Axel was having a hard time learning radio, he said he'd bring over a friend.

"He's only a soda-jerker in an East Side drug store," he explained. "But he knows plenty about radio. He used to be an operator with the German Army."

That was how Felix Jahnke came into the spy set-up as Axel Wheeler-Hill's assistant.

And then, when Axel said he was ready to have a short-wave set built, Reuper had another suggestion:

"I know the man to help you. He's with us. He's now working as a commercial photographer but he knows all about building a set."

"I certainly appreciate all you're doing for me," Axel said.

"Those are my orders," Reuper replied. "We've got to work together." Then he quoted, "Today, we rule Germany. Tomorrow, we rule the whole world."

So Axel was introduced to Josef August Klein, who said he'd have no trouble at all building a set according to Axel's specifications. It would cost about $200. Axel told him to go ahead.

In the meantime, Axel found time to spend hours prowling along the Brooklyn waterfront. His wolfish eyes were constantly on the alert for anything that looked like munitions going aboard freighters. When he was too busy, he would send Jahnke.

Between them, they began sending reports to Germany, sometimes by airmail letters via neutral countries and sometimes by ship courier. At first, Axel doubted whether these slow means of communication would be able to tip off the Nazi U-boat fleet in time. And as he read the newspaper reports, he saw that many of the ships had escaped. And this put him in high spirits. It was great fun. It was almost as if he himself, Axel Wheeler-Hill, was firing the torpedo. And how much more fun it would be when he had his radio set working. Then none would escape!

But there were many times when he read of a vessel

on which he had "put the finger" being sunk by a submarine or air-bombed to the bottom.

Meanwhile, the FBI was getting its own radio station into shape. Sebold had promised Hamburg that he would go on the air on May 15th, and he didn't want to disappoint the Gestapo bosses.

But early on that day, he received a letter from Metzger.

It read:

Dear Harry—I absolutely must see you at noon, May 16th. Didn't you receive my last letter? I'm supposed to give you greetings from the man in Hamburg. Meet me at the Eagle Bar, near Pier 53.

Neither Sebold nor his FBI coaches could imagine what was up, but they decided to find out before going on with anything else.

On the next day, Sebold found Metzger in the bar, sipping a glass of wine in a dark corner.

"What's the matter?" Sebold demanded. "Is anything wrong?"

Metzger shrugged. "I don't know. It's Aufzug, the ship's baker. He's brought you some money and instructions. But something seems to have scared him. He was afraid to come near you. He wants me to tell you to meet him tomorrow night at Columbus Circle."

Much puzzled, Sebold went on the next night to Columbus Circle, at 59th Street and Broadway. As usual, in the big open space around the statue of Christopher Columbus there were speechmakers. Each with his little group around him. Some of the speakers were arguing on behalf of Atheism; some were shouting loudly their ideas on government and the rights of man.

Sebold found Aufzug trying to look like a man intensely interested in the harangue a speaker was making on Communism. He plucked his shoulder.

Aufzug turned to him quickly and said, "Let's go to a quiet café."

[58]

When they had sat down, Sebold inquired. "Why so nervous—anything wrong?"

"I'm pretty sure somebody has been following me," said the courier. Sebold smiled to himself. Of course somebody had been following the man. The FBI's surveillance men weren't asleep.

"But I've shaken him off," said Aufzug. He handed over an envelope containing $240. "It's for the Sperry man who wanted more money. You are to let me know when he will have more material ready."

So, the next day, Sebold went out to Merrick, Long Island, and looked up Everett Roeder, the very respectable engineer who was a Nazi spy at the Sperry Gyroscope plant. Roeder took the money greedily.

"Chicken feed!" he snorted. "But I suppose I'll have to prime the pump. Tell them I'm working on something important. I'll have it ready sometime next month."

There were some last-minute experimental tests with the FBI's radio transmitter on Long Island's north shore.

At six o'clock on the evening of May 22nd, three men sat in a room of the bungalow. Everything was ready—one G-man had his hand on the transmitter's switch; the other was rewording the message to be sent, for the last time. Sebold had the code book, *All This and Heaven Too*, ready.

Then one G-man handed the message to his operator colleague and nodded.

Nine

THE MOMENT THAT the FBI had been waiting for had arrived. For the first time in history, two rival secret service organizations were to match wits over the air. It was the FBI, based on intelligence and legal methods against the Nazi Gestapo, based on cunning and brutality.

The Special Agent's finger began tapping the key. Out into the ether, and over the Atlantic, went his call letters, "CQDXvW-2." Over and over for two minutes. But there was no answer from the receiving set.

"Their instructions said to rest for ten minutes, then try again," he said, as he shut off the transmitter.

When ten minutes had passed, he tried again. And once more, he rested. The eyes of the other two men watched his face to see if he was getting anything through the headphones.

And then he exclaimed, "They're answering! They're answering! Station AOR is answering Station CQDXvW-2."

Then he began scribbling down the message that was coming in, even though it was also being recorded on a wax disc.

A minute later, he snapped off the set and removed his headphones. "They've signed off," he said.

With pencils and paper, the men began figuring out what the message meant in their codebook.

The first words they figured out were "*Sehr gut! Sehr gut!*"

Sebold roared with laughter. "That means—Very good! Very good!"

Then came the rest of the message: "Grand work, old bean, keep it up."

Sebold's coach grinned. "I hope to tell you we will— and how! This is only the beginning."

Transatlantic radio reception was bad the two following days. But on the third day, May 27th, 1940, the ether cleared. And again the three men gathered in the hideaway bungalow on Long Island's lonely north shore where the FBI had installed its secret radio station.

They had high hopes. Their first air contact with the Gestapo's station over in Germany had been a success. And the Gestapo had congratulated Bill Sebold. It evidently had fallen hook, line and sinker; believed that the Long Island station was being run by Nazis. Tonight, the three hoped to get their first earful of important spy ring business by air.

The men gathered around the apparatus of CQD-XvW-2 were Sebold, the stolid-faced big fellow who was a naturalized American citizen, and who had offered to help the FBI smash the espionage ring shortly after the Gestapo "argued" him into turning Nazi spy by threatening his life and that of his relatives still in Germany; a Special Agent who had been assigned to coach Sebold in counter-espionage work; and another Special Agent who operated the transmitter which the confident Nazis believed was being run by Sebold.

Again on this night, at the appointed time, the G-man began tapping his key, calling, listening, calling. And finally, into his headphones and on to the wax disc that was turning the air conversations into permanent evidence, came the dot-dash coded reply sent out by Station AOR over in Hitler's land.

The G-men and Sebold quickly went to work with their complicated "square code" which had been taught to Sebold by the Gestapo—involving the use of words in the best-seller, *All This And Heaven Too*. And this was the message AOR had sent:

Send only two times per week. We are prepared to receive and send daily. Furnish days you expect to send. For your security also send at other times. We are prepared to receive at 7 A.M. and 5 P.M. Call signal only three letters. No CQ. Furnish frequency outside amateur band.

An answer was immediately sent to AOR, giving the details requested.

[61]

On the following night, the Gestapo station seemed to have revised its plans a little. It sent the following message:

Your signal is very weak. Can you improve it? I will send Tuesdays and Thursdays, at 1 and 5 P.M. E.S.T. After that will listen daily except Saturday night and Sunday. Saturday, 12 noon, OK. Will furnish you new frequency later.

The FBI made haste to add more power to its station, so that there would be no further complaint about weak signals.

It was clear why the Gestapo wanted Sebold to change his sending schedule "for your security." It thought Sebold was running an outlaw station. And it didn't want American "radio-detectives" of our FCC to locate his transmitter with "direction-finding" equipment.

As it happened, an FCC radio-sleuth did go to work, but not on the matter of the FBI station, concerning which the FCC had been informed. This investigator belonged to the FCC's National Defense Operations Section. In order to help the FBI build up its case, he was assigned to prove with scientific evidence that AOR was actually in Germany.

He did this by conducting exhaustive "direction-finding" tests throughout our country from Government monitor stations which listened in when AOR was sending. It was a matter, largely, of then drawing straight lines. An FCC station in Massachusetts, for instance, would draw a line showing the direction from which AOR's message was coming. The same would be done by an FCC station in Texas. Where the two lines met showed where the AOR broadcast was originating.

Most of the time the broadcasting was from Hamburg, Germany, home base of the American branch of the German spy ring. But often it moved to some other place in Nazi territory for a while. This, it turned out, was to avoid destruction in British air raids.

[62]

There was one other point. The Gestapo station was an "outlaw," because of the call letters it had taken for itself. Under international radio regulations, a transmitter was forbidden to use either "A" or "B" in its call letters. But Station AOR, being a Nazi outfit, of course didn't worry much about international laws.

After the matter of sending schedules was settled over the air, the FBI sent its first "business" message. Sebold had again visited Lilly Stein, the pretty artist's model the Gestapo sent to New York to collect spy material from other members of the ring. She said she was prepared to turn over material to him, but pointed out that she was flat broke. She absolutely needed some spy ring pay.

So the message was sent to AOR:

Stein destitute. Got new contact, but must have money at once.

But beauteous Lilly had made the Gestapo weary with her whining for money. Back came AOR's message:

Need urgently from all friends monthly production of airplane factories, exports to all countries, especially England and France; number, type, date of delivery by steamer or air; armature (this apparently referred to the armor with which the plane or vessel carrying the exports was equipped; so that the Nazis would know what type of torpedoes or bombs to use) and armament; payment, cash and carry, or credit.

Rose has $200 for you, not for Stein. Greetings.

This convinced the FBI that the hoax it was perpetrating on the Gestapo was really working. For this was apparently the beginning of real spy business by air. Sebold didn't know who "Rose" was, but it was evidently some courier who was bringing him $200. The Gestapo figured that the $1,000 it had already given him had been spent by now.

So Sebold, with his heavy-footed trudge and poker

face, went out calling on those spy ring members he already knew, announcing that his radio station was now ready for any information they wanted to send to Nikolaus, the boss back in Hamburg, and telling them of the order to get busy on warplane data.

The understandable caution with which he was at first received was now gone. The ring's professional spy, Frederick Duquesne, said he was in the midst of getting a lot of good stuff, and it would be ready soon. Others were similarly optimistic.

Meanwhile, even sad-faced Herman Lang had begun opening up to Sebold.

So far, the FBI had only strong suspicions that Lang, when he visited Germany in 1938, had delivered the bombsight's mechanical secrets to the Gestapo. As will be recalled on Sebold's first visit to Lang's home in Queens, the latter had shut up like a clam, refusing even to admit that he recognized the password, "Rantzau, Berlin, Hamburg."

But when Sebold called again, one day in June, 1940, Lang was more talkative. Sebold wanted to know what the other intended to do about the Gestapo's orders that he return to Germany via Siberia. On the other visit, Lang had declared that he had no desire or intention of going to Germany.

But now he said, "You will have to fix it up. An easier route must be arranged. My wife's health isn't good, and a trip across Siberia would be too hard on her."

"Then it isn't," Sebold prodded, "because you fear you won't have your expenses paid?"

Lang shrugged. "No, not that. To be truthful, I haven't yet received a cent for what I did. But I'm not worrying. I know I'll be taken care of."

A week later, he had another reason for declining to make the trip. This time, it was a pretty good reason.

"I've just been fingerprinted at the plant," he said.

Sebold clucked sympathetically. "Do you think they suspect?"

"I don't know. But I don't think so. Everybody was fingerprinted because it's a defense plant. The main trouble is that I can't leave the country. I asked about it and was told that nobody with a vital job like mine would be allowed to leave."

So far, Lang had not admitted in so many words that he had sold the Norden bombsight to the Nazis. But Sebold was patient.

He came back a month later. Lang had company, whom he introduced as his cousin and the latter's child. Taking Sebold to one side, he whispered, "Don't discuss our business in their presence."

When the visitors had gone, Sebold inquired, "Doesn't your cousin know about the affair?"

"No," said the sad-faced traitor. "I'm the only man who knows about this American technical secret. But something must be done. I cannot go to Germany. And I refuse to do anything more till I get paid for the bombsight."

So—it had come out at last!

"I was offered $10,000," he continued. "And it's about time I got paid."

"You mean you're afraid they'll cheat you?"

"They'd better not! I met Chancellor Hitler personally. And Air Marshal Goering told me that the bombsight was the most important thing in the world. If there's any cheating tried, I'll write to him personally. So get busy, Herr Sawyer, and see that I'm paid."

Sebold got busy, gladly. He radioed a message to AOR that Lang was getting impatient about payment.

Soon there came the coded reply:

Tell Lang that 10,000 marks are here awaiting him.

Sebold took the message to the Norden spy. The latter frowned. "But I was to be paid 10,000 *dollars,* not *marks.* At the present rate of exchange, this means only about $4,000."

Sebold shrugged helplessly.

[65]

Then Lang said gutturally, "All right. I'll accept. Now you explain to them that there is thick air here. The heat is on. I am not allowed to go to Germany."

"Then you want the money sent to you?"

Lang pondered. "No," he replied. "One of these days, Germany will fight America, and win. American money will be worthless. I want that money to be given into the care of my sister."

So back went a message to AOR:

Lang requests that the money be deposited, in marks, in the Dresdener Bank, in the name of his sister, Johanna Lang, who should be notified. He cannot come himself. The air is too thick.

There was some delay in getting a reply. Lang grew impatient, and sent a note to "Harry Sawyer"—the name which Sebold had been told to use by the Gestapo:

Dear Mr. Sawyer—I must see you. Come to my home.

But meanwhile, AOR had sent its reply. Lang's instructions had been complied with.

Sebold took the message to the Norden spy, who shrugged and said, "Well, it's about time."

They talked about the Norden bombsight.

"How does it compare with the Sperry bombsight now being put out in America and sold to Britain?" Sebold asked.

"That's not in my line," Lang said. "I'm not an aviator. But what's the difference? All our side has to do is shoot down a British bomber equipped with a Sperry sight—and our engineers will quickly know all its secrets."

"Then why was your information so valuable?"

"That's easy. Because, through me, our side knew all about the Norden sight long before the war began. Don't you see?"

He added that he had dug up some new material that would be valuable, and proceeded to give Sebold the

Norden Company's monthly production figures. "Send it over on your radio."

But that was one message which Sebold and his FBI colleagues took good care *not* to send to Hamburg.

Meanwhile, there were plenty of other members of the spy ring who also kept Sebold busy. One was the artist's model, Lilly Stein, who finally turned up with some stuff to prove that her talk about a "valuable contact" wasn't just a myth. It was she who first brought Edmund Carl Heine to the FBI's attention.

And very luckily, because Heine was probably doing more than any other one man to keep the Nazis informed of the entire American aviation picture. His was the kind of reports that Hitler himself would study before deciding on a next move against America.

He was more intelligent than most of the spies. And he was no Nazi crackpot. He was a shrewd, successful American businessman who knew all the ropes and could move about with ease.

He was a stocky man with a mole on one cheek, a comfortable family man with a smile for everybody and eager to show you snapshots of his wife and three children. A real go-getter. A crack salesman. Although born in Germany, he had long ago lost his accent and was a naturalized American cizen.

He was twenty-three years old in 1914, when he emigrated to the United States. At first, he worked as a hardware salesman. Then he got a job in the Detroit tractor division of the Ford Motor Company.

He rose through the ranks. In 1928, owing to his knowledge of German conditions and talent as a salesman, he got his big chance—he was sent to Germany to be managing director of Ford's German subsidiary, with headquarters in Cologne.

He boomed Fords and before long he was pulling down a salary of $30,000 a year plus expenses. But troubles arose when the Nazis came into power in 1933. There were boycotts and whispering campaigns. Germany's own automobile manufacturers called on Germans to be loyal, to buy home-made products, to spurn anything American.

Heine returned to Detroit in 1934 to make a personal report on the company's German troubles. Then he returned to Germany, ordered to see if he couldn't pacify the Nazis. But he failed in that and had to resign in 1935.

His next job represented quite a comedown in salary —he was made the Chrysler Motor Company's sales agent for Germany and Spain, at $8,400 a year.

But even this job wouldn't be a very successful one, he figured shrewdly, when the Spanish Civil War broke out and all Europe began arming. Automobiles turned into a luxury that few Europeans could afford.

Heine was all business. The oath he had taken in becoming an American citizen meant nothing to him. If he couldn't do business with America, then he could do it with Germany.

And that's what he proceeded to do. He began peddling his offers to the Nazi war machine. He was grabbed up.

Hitler had promised the German people a "People's Car," a cheap automobile which everybody would be able to afford. And he had begun building his famous network of highways, along which Germans could drive their "People's Car." As a matter of fact, they never got it.

And so it turned out to be another one of Hitler's broken promises. The highways were really intended for the mechanized divisions with which Hitler planned to blitzkrieg his neighbors. And the *Volks Wagen-werke*, "People's Car" factory, was secretly turned over to the manufacture of warplanes and tanks.

It was to the *Volks Wagen-werke* that Heine was summoned for a conference. Here, he met two very important gentlemen. One was a Dr. Porsch, head of the plant. The other was a Dr. Wirtz, who was interested in the aviation branch.

They quickly made it plain what they wanted. Heine

was to return to America and make comprehensive, secret reports on the American aviation industry so that Germany would know what she was facing, and what to do about it. He was to report on the latest in warplanes—from guns to superchargers. He was to keep Germany informed on how many planes we were turning out, and how many we planned to turn out. He was to give special attention to the possibility of our automobile plants being turned to warplane production.

Then he sat down with Gestapo officials and was instructed how to get his reports into Nazi hands. He was given the aliases he should use and a list of thirty "letter boxes"—Nazi agents scattered all over the world who would relay his information to Germany.

Leaving his wife and children in Germany, Heine took the usual German spy route to the United States—by train to Genoa, Italy, where he boarded the steamer *Manhattan* of the United States Line.

He remained in New York for a couple of weeks, looking up old friends in the motors industry and pumping them for information. On Memorial Day, 1940, he went to Detroit—to stay with his brother until his own family came back from Germany.

Grass wasn't growing under the go-getter's feet. We find him shortly in Bridgeport, Connecticut. In that city a young fellow named Harry Thorell, an aviation enthusiast and photographer, had set himself up in business as "Thorell's Aircraft Photo Service."

And he had put an ad in an aviation magazine, advertising his wares.

Into Thorell's home strode genial Heine, carrying the magazine in his hand, by way of introduction.

"I'd like some pictures of military planes," Heine explained. "You see, with all this war talk going on, I feel pretty dumb. I'd like to be able to carry on an intelligent conversation about military aviation. I know a lot about cars, but planes are different. So I thought I'd buy some of your pictures as a starter."

[69]

"Sure," Thorell said. "How many would you want?"

"Oh, about fifty, if you've got that many."

"Sure—it'll cost you five bucks. Do you want to wait —I'll pick out some."

"Oh, no," said Heine. "Just send them to the Hotel Governor Clinton, New York City, where I usually stay."

He knew that the pictures he'd get, in themselves, wouldn't be important. They'd be common, oft-published photos with nothing secret about them. But he wanted them to be only a starter in pumping Thorell.

On that same day, while still in Bridgeport at the Hotel Stratfield, he wrote a letter to Thorell:

This is simply to confirm the order I placed with you. I want to emphasize that I am interested only in modern planes that are now in use, under construction, or that are planned to be produced. Also give the names and addresses of their manufacturers. Of the various concerns, I'd like to know the names of the five or six biggest. I'm also interested in anything you might know about stratosphere planes.

You see, I'd like to talk intelligently about the matter, if it is possible for a layman to do so. If $5 cannot pay for my education as desired, will you please tell me frankly how much more?

All this left young Thorell pretty puzzled. The man was asking him things he didn't know much about. So he sent the photographs. But he also had presence of mind enough to let the FBI know about Heine's aviation curiosity.

Meanwhile, Thorell's method of reaching the public had given Heine an idea. He had an advertisement inserted in the next issue of the magazine, *Popular Aviation*. In the ad he said he wanted to get in touch with an aviation engineer, aviator or high-grade mechanic who would be able to teach him basic knowledge about modern airplanes. In this way he hoped to snare somebody who had "inside dope" on Uncle Sam's warplanes.

But the ad wouldn't appear until the magazine's August issue. In the meantime, Heine wasn't loafing. In fact, the amount of stuff he picked up in a hurry was astonishing. Much of it came from a careful reading of articles in technical magazines. More of it came from his successful pumping of persons who knew what was going on in aviation.

As in the cases of most spies, we know more about their attempts that failed, and less about the times when they successfully covered up their tracks.

On June 5th, only a month after Heine landed in the United States, Lilly Stein received a long report from "Heinrich," the name assigned to him in the spy ring.

It began with a description of the kind of motors used in our warplanes. He listed the plants putting out Diesel motors, but pointed out that this type was still pretty much in the experimental stage, and most American warplanes still relied on radial air-cooled engines.

After listing the various airplane companies that used Pratt & Whitney engines, he went on to sing the praises of the Allison motor, manufactured by General Motors. This was the motor, he pointed out, that was being put in the American Army's newest sensation, the Bell Airacobra—the fighting plane equipped with machine guns and cannon which had a cruising speed of 400 miles per hour and a flying range of 1,000 miles.

"This ship," he wrote, "is the sensation of the industry. It is called 'The Killer.'"

Heine was a shrewd judge of military aircraft. That Airacobra—the Army's P-39—was later to prove itself one of Uncle Sam's main weapons in the air.

Lilly Stein quickly telephoned Sebold to come to her apartment. When he arrived, she handed him Heine's report and said, "It must be sent to Germany immediately."

"All right," he said heavily, "I will make a micro of it and send it on. Is there anything else?"

Yes, she said, and explained she'd like to make a trip to California, if Hamburg was willing.

[71]

So the FBI radio station rapped out a message to AOR over in Hitler's land:

. . . . Stein wants to go to California for two months with her cousin. She asks if she can make contacts or work for you there. She got letter from Heinrich, Detroit, regarding plane motors. How shall I send it and other things I have?

Seeb.

The answer was for Lilly to stay in New York, and for Sebold to send his information by air.

This was done—but only after the FBI had edited down Heine's report, removing all of the technical details that would do Germany any good. To make up for the stuff they removed, the FBI men added some hokum that would wreck any German warplane built according to Heine's specifications.

A week later, Lilly had another Heine report for Sebold. It contained additions to the previous one and went on to give the low-down on American high-altitude ships, how they were built and also where the vital factories were, so that spies could get jobs in those factories for the purpose of stealing the secrets or committing sabotage.

The FBI did some doctoring on this report, after which it, too, was sent to Germany.

But an even bigger and more important report—consisting of seven typewritten pages—was soon afterward received by Sebold through Lilly Stein.

In this one, Heine really "went to town" with information that Germany badly needed. It was dated July 1st, 1940.

As of this date the U. S. has shipped a total of 2,950 fighting planes to England, including several hundred bombers. Of this number, 400 were handed over by the U. S. Army and Navy. There are 7,450 more planes on order, including 4,250 bombers that should be completed within eighteen months. Of the ships on order, at least 3,600 are to be equipped with powerful Allison motors.

The manufacture of big engines has been the principal bottleneck in plane manufacture, but this bad condition is being overcome.

By the end of 1941, it is entirely likely that the U. S. will be equipped to turn out 50,000 fighting planes of all types. There is no doubt in my mind that in six months this country can in time produce a swarm of planes. Henry Ford has stated he could build 1,000 planes a day by the end of 1941 if he got the specifications and the go-ahead signal. I am sure he could do it. Fortunately for us, that genius of industry refuses to build planes for any of the warring nations; would build them, he claims, only for national defense. But the General Motors and Chrysler Corporations are not bound by such restrictions.

How Heine wormed his information can be seen from evidence which the FBI was to get later.

Norman Davidson, assistant contract administrator of the Consolidated Aircraft Corporation, San Diego, California, had written a trade magazine article declaring that Consolidated had put a plane into the air nine months after its designers first began working on the plans.

To him came a letter from Heine:

As an engineer, I would be interested in more details. For instance, how many man-hours were required in this splendid achievement. . . ? Of course, if any of my questions cannot be answered for military reasons, please ignore them.

Davidson sent Heine some publicity releases and general information, but pointed out that other matters were Consolidated's secrets.

Encouraged by Davidson's politeness, Heine sent back another letter, peppering the man with all kinds of questions about aviation technicalities, especially in regard to bombing planes. "And which company is the biggest producer of planes?" he inquired. Needless to say, Davidson had sense enough to make only a vague reply.

Heine knew the value of piecing together bits of information to be found in aviation magazines. Several articles which had appeared in the March issue of *Aero-Digest* had been referred to him. He tried to buy that back issue from the publishers. When that failed, he went to the Detroit Public Library and made photostats of the articles.

At the same time, in order to get a special aircraft number of the magazine *Machinery,* he sent in his $5 and subscribed to the publication for the entire year.

Then we find him pumping Neil Caward of *Aeronautical Publications,* trying to learn the number of men employed in various divisions of America's aviation industry. Caward guessed that there were 75,000 men so employed at that time.

Next he wrote a postcard to Charles H. Romer, President of the Industrial Commission at Paterson, New Jersey.

I am asking you on behalf of some friends who are working on a patent for a new type of airplane engine to send me your booklet entitled "Industrial Advantages of a Paterson Location."

Romer, thinking this was simply an ordinary request by somebody who was considering the site for a factory, sent the pamphlet to the inquirer at 4447 Baldwin Avenue, Detroit.

Back came Heine's wily answer,

Thank you for your prompt reply. In order to get a more complete picture of the Paterson situation, I would now like to know how many men are employed in aviation factories in the Paterson area, and how many plants there are. Your otherwise instructive pamphlet does not seem to contain that information.

Romer complied:

We wish to advise you that the Wright Aeronautical Corporation employs more than 10,000 persons in their Paterson factory. This does not include the Curtiss propeller division, which covers 100,000 square feet and is building a large addition. Many others are in the area, such as Bendix, Firestone, etc. . . . Please advise us what your specific interest is and we will be glad to be of further service.

But Heine didn't like the sound of the query as to his "specific interest" and thought it best to be satisfied with what he had learned.

Meanwhile, he had begun to receive some answers to his ad in *Popular Aviation,* in which he wanted an expert to teach him the fundamentals of aviation.

One was from Claude Brewster, Toledo, Ohio, who said that he was himself building an airplane. But Heine thought the man was only an amateur and didn't reply.

Then he got one from an aged man, Albert H. Morris, living at the Drake Hotel, Atlantic City.

"In reply to your advertisement," Morris wrote, "I can teach you more about aviation than anybody alive. I am the oldest man in that business."

Heine wondered if it was a crackpot letter, but thought it was worth answering:

. . . Here is what I am after. I am 45 years of age and an old man in the automobile business but think it is about time I learned something about aviation because it is the big business of the future. I am not a mechanic. I have worked my way up, after many years of hard labor, to an executive post in the auto industry. In regard to airplanes, I am looking for someone who can teach me why and what makes the thing fly. I don't want just talk. I have been reading much of the technical literature, but it has nothing for me. Are you able to teach me about modern developments in aviation?

For some reason or other, Morris didn't reply.

But Heine didn't worry, because his ad had turned up a really top-notch prospect—Boyd M. Aldrich of Washington, D. C.

Heine felt that here was a man who would know plenty of "inside" stuff. In his letter, Aldrich pointed out that he had been a civilian and Navy aviator for fourteen years; had done technical aviation work at the Bureau of Standards and was now an expert plane mechanic and parachute rigger known at all the airports in and around Washington.

So Heine got into his car and drove to the capital city. From a drug store he phoned Aldrich. "I got your letter," he said, "and thought I'd look you up because I'm driving through Washington, anyway. I'm at 14th and K Streets—you'll know me by the bright red necktie I'm wearing."

When Aldrich arrived, the spy explained his predicament.

"I'm in the auto business, but I'm abysmally ignorant about airplanes. Why, I was never so ashamed of myself as a few days ago when I gave my little boy a present— a model airplane. He wanted to know all kinds of things about it, and I had to admit I didn't know.

"Besides," he added confidentially, "when the war's over, I happen to know that Henry Ford's going to build light civilian planes on a mass-production basis. I'd like to know enough to apply for a job selling them."

So they toured the Washington airports, examined planes and discussed manufacturing costs.

"I think you'll do," said Heine. "Right now, I'm too busy to stay. But here's $20 as a starter. For a beginner, I'd like you to send me a pretty complete picture of the number and location of plane factories in the country, and how many workers they have."

But when Heine had gone, Aldrich began thinking it over, looked up a friend in the CAA and told him about Heine's assignment.

His friend agreed the entire business looked suspicious. And as a result, Aldrich went to FBI headquarters with his story.

It was a very welcome one. His account of the man Edmund Carl Heine, living in Detroit, and prowling around for plane information, fitted beautifully the man

"Heinrich" who had been mailing reports from Detroit to Lilly Stein, and the man, Heine, who had bought plane photos from Thorell.

Quickly, FBI shadowers began hanging around the Detroit address. But Heine didn't come home for a while yet. He had other matters to keep him busy in the East.

He drove to a suburb of Baltimore and dropped in on a distant relative—Mrs. Spittel, who was a cousin of Heine's wife. Of her three sons, Gordon Spittel turned out to be the apple of Heine's eye.

Need I say more than to point out that Gordon had been working at the Glenn Martin Company's plant near Baltimore—builders of the famous American bomber?

And naturally, cousin Heine, that week-end, wanted very much to see the sights. Gordon, entirely innocent, was very agreeable. So he took Heine where the man wanted to go.

"I've heard a lot about Baltimore's wonderful waterfront," Heine said as a starter. So they went there, then had a view of the city's airport, then went up to the top of the Baltimore Trust Company's building—Baltimore's tallest structure, from where a spy could memorize the entire landscape—and then out for a tour of the Martin plant. And all the time, Heine chatted pleasantly of aviation matters.

A few days later the Spittels got a letter from him, full of thanks for their hospitality.

. . . I'm sure you have a fine set of boys. By the way, will you please ask Gordon (because it has slipped my mind) whether it was 12,000 men working at the Martin plant, three shifts a day, or was it 4,000 men per shift—which would make it a total of 12,000 for the day? And how many planes do they put out a day? Does he happen to know also how many in the Fairchild plant? This will all be useful to me if I go into the airplane business—because the auto business is pretty bad these days. In return, count on me to do Gordon a favor in anything.

[77]

Gordon sent an answer which didn't tell very much because the youth didn't know the details which fact-greedy Heine wanted. In return, Gordon got a reply:

. . . It isn't necessary to send any more data. I've subscribed to several aviation publications which fill the bill. Many thanks.

From then on, Heine made several more spying trips which we know about, but eventually he seemed to become suspicious that he was being watched, and began lying low.

Meanwhile, the rest of the spies were as busy as bees. And Sebold was even busier than that, trying to "help" them, and at the same time keep the FBI fully informed of all that was happening. Here is a chronology of some of the things that happened from June, 1940, on.

On June 3rd, two weeks before France fell, the FBI's secret radio station received a message from the Gestapo's station, intended for Sebold, who the Nazis still believed was their agent:

Thanks for reports. Observe *Normandie.* Use for calling only last three letters, but not W-2, for your safety.

The *Normandie,* of course, was the famous French liner which the Nazis hoped to capture in mid-ocean.

Nine days later, Sebold got a phone call from Metzger, the ring's spy courier who was a butcher on the *Manhattan,* to meet him at Columbus Circle. Metzger handed over one of the tiny negatives—the size of a postage stamp—which was known as a micro.

It contained a batch of new instructions for the ring's free-lance spy Duquesne—the man who was now working for the Nazis after forty years of conniving and espionage all over the world.

The FBI enlarged the micro and had a look at it before Sebold delivered it to Duquesne. It was a request for information about American warplane shipments abroad and especially about the Pratt & Whitney airplane engine plants—where they were located, how the motors were built, and the personal history of each employee. This last was obviously in hopes of finding men who could be bought, or threatened into becoming Nazi agents.

Then Everett Roeder, the engineer who was stealing secrets from his employer, the Sperry Gyroscope Company, popped up again—not knowing that the FBI had been watching him.

He was seen taking a blueprint out of the plant on the night of June 13th. That same night, he phoned Sebold.

They met the next day at the Hempstead, Long Island, railroad station, where Roeder turned over his document.

It turned out to be a harmless, complicated drawing of an electrical mechanism, and it was allowed to go to Germany. Sebold gave it to one of the ship couriers, Erich Strunck, the steward on the *Siboney*.

Ten

OTHER COURIERS WERE constantly coming to Sebold to give him instructions and pick up material he had ready. And the FBI saw to it that they were given plenty of harmless junk. By watching the couriers, the FBI put two more suspects on the spy conspiracy list—two men who were constantly meeting in dark corners with Metzger and Aufzug. The two were Alfred Brokhoff, a mechanic employed on piers along the New York waterfront, and Heinrich Clausing, a seaman aboard the S.S. *Argentina*.

Then Duquesne sent Sebold a letter declaring that orders were fine, but what he wanted was some more pay.

On June 29th, the FBI's station received a message for Sebold which, he knew, would gladden the hearts of some of the spies. Money was coming. It also told him what to do with some of the material he was receiving which was too lengthy to transmit by radio:

Deliver all material through Metzger to H. Duarte at Lisbon, Duos Nacoes. Password on meeting, "Sesan Greek Franz." Duarte will hand over $500 for Roeder, $300 for you, $300 for Lily and $250 for Dunn. Distribution of money by you. Don't borrow any money for Lily. All should report military and technical information on deliveries to England. Hearty greetings.

By "Lily" was meant Lilly Stein. And Dunn was one of Duquesne's aliases.

On top of this came another message showing that the Nazis, after smashing France, were contemplating an invasion of England. To do this, they had to construct an "invasion weather" map—and they needed to know weather conditions far enough away to enable them to make forecasts. So they demanded:

Report weather conditions daily, barometric pressure, wind direction, velocity, temperature, visibility, height of clouds.

Then the courier Metzger began worrying—suppose when his ship, the *Manhattan,* stopped at Lisbon, none of the crew would be allowed ashore? This would make it impossible for him to deliver his material or pick up the $1,350 he was supposed to bring back to Sebold.

So the following radio message was sent to AOR:

Metzger says if no one comes off ship, Duarte should try to come in small boat as peddler to port side midship, lower porthole, from which appears antenna or stick with tin can tied to string between 17 and 20 o'clock Greenwich Time.

But Metzger's worry had been useless. He went ashore, met Herr Dobler, who ran a German "importing" firm in Lisbon as a cover-up for his activities as Gestapo agent "Duarte." Before long Metzger was back in New York turning the $1,350 over to Sebold. Then he handed Sebold a separate packet containing $1,500.

"He told me to tell you," Metzger explained, "that the $1,500 is for sending over the latest American bombsight. But not the Norden, because we have that one already."

So Sebold passed out the money to the spies he was supposed to, but the $300 for himself, and the $1,500 for the bombsight was kept by the FBI for the American Government. Eventually, the sum totaled over $22,000—money sent by the Gestapo in various ways to its pride and joy, William Sebold.

And the Gestapo still kept worrying about the growing American air force. It couldn't get enough information about the number of Allison motors we were able to put into warplanes:

How many Allison motors made in series in Indianapolis have been delivered up to now and where? How many Allison motors manufactured in General Motors works before Autumn, 1939?

Then the FBI wondered if perhaps it had not been sending too much "baloney" to the Nazis, because there came this order from AOR:

[81]

Confine your radio messages to pure military and technical inquiries. However, listen to us daily.

Meanwhile, spurred on by the payment he had received and eager to get more, the ring's professional spy, Duquesne, was stirring himself to much activity. Where and how he got his information was a mystery—but he was an old hand at the spy game, and he even knew how to imagine plenty—if it sounded good and would bring him some Gestapo pay.

On July 24th, he ordered Sebold to send the following message to AOR:

Dunn says four battleships of Texas class and ten destroyers going Caribbean to scout for England. Six hundred reservists, 600 enlisted men. Todd Drydock has contracted to put laminated anti-bomb deck on U. S. destroyers—20 new destroyers, 20 World War destroyers. Explosion takes places before bomb reaches lamination. U. S. conservative papers favor union between U. S. and Britain.

On the next day, Duquesne had some more stuff to be radioed:

Dunn says investigation being made by Capt. Coon of a mask and canister said to be able to stop chlorine.

Bullitt, FDR, British Diplomatic Corps met at Hyde Park, discussed Hitler's message.

Army advisory board thinking of stopping production Garand rifle because of poor results.

By "Bullitt" he was referring to William Bullitt who had been our Ambassador to France. The Hitler message was the one in which the Nazi Fuehrer gave his "last ultimatum" to England, after having crushed France.

Back came a message from AOR:

Please repeat first sentence of your Message 36 concerning chlorine. Who is Capt. Coon? Does it concern chlorine?

As a result, Sebold checked with Duquesne and replied:

Repeating 36. Dunn says investigation being made by Capt. Coon of a mask and canister said to be able to stop chlorine. It concerns chlorine. Coon is an American of German descent in the U. S. Army.

Then the FBI gave the Gestapo something else to worry about. It sent a message on July 29th:

I am sending you microphotos by mail. How shall I send you accumulated bulk material? U. S. Lines no longer go to Europe.

The Gestapo answered that one:

A new friend will arrive mid-September. Password: 'Bring greetings from Jack Rosen.' You will reply: 'Is he still with the Swift people?' He will bring you $1,000. Distribution details we will give you later. Regarding yesterday's inquiry, ship via Clipper or Export Line to Portugal.

And so the spy ring's stewards and other seamen on American Export Line ships, and on trans-Atlantic Clipper planes took over the brunt of the courier work for a while.

Then the Gestapo wirelessed another task:

Airplane carrier *Saratoga* is said to have delivered large number of planes to Halifax. Tell all friends to get details about this and make all effort to obtain more data regarding deliveries to England.

The FBI men chuckled because the "friends" were doing the best they could—the trouble was that the FBI station wasn't transmitting this vital information. And to give the Gestapo a bum steer, they waited a few days, then replied:

Best available information is *Saratoga* still on West Coast and did not take any airplanes to Halifax.

Time and again, the Gestapo became alarmed or suspicious. It sent a message telling Sebold to warn Lilly Stein to be more careful in the letters she was sending to Germany.

[83]

Then it dashed a wireless message to Sebold:

Achtung! Caution! Friend reports you are under surveillance. You must remain off air for two weeks. We
will be ready to receive when you return.

And the FBI kept wondering how much longer the
"super-minds" of the "super-Gestapo" would go on sending their "secret messages" to—the FBI.

The Gestapo's scare passed, and AOR sent the following message:

On August 20th, begin sending again three days week-
ly. First week, Wednesday and Friday. Second week,
Tuesday, Thursday. Third week, Monday, Wednesday,
Friday. You change your frequency daily and furnish
new frequency in message. Our frequency remains the
same. No new code system.

Another way in which the Gestapo demonstrated its
optimism was in the habit it had of asking for any secret
it happened to want. It just didn't seem to realize that
FBI Director Hoover's recommendations were causing
guards to watch our defense plants like hawks—and that
a spy couldn't simply walk in whenever he cared to and
get what he wanted. Here's an AOR request of September 4th:

We want drawings and newest data concerning hydraulic fuel pump. Even so of newest bombsight. See
article in New York *Herald Tribune* of June 16. Obtain
details.

On the other hand, the spies uncovered many things
they weren't specifically asked to get. Hartwig Kleiss, the
chief cook on the *Manhattan,* came into Sebold's office
one September day and handed him this report to be
forwarded:

I have just spent some time around the shipyards of
Norfolk, Virginia. I understand that the so-called ghost
fleet there is being prepared for use by England. There
is a 35,000-ton battleship on which construction has just

begun. Progress is slow. The gang of men of German origin was held together very briefly. I was stopped many times in my walk around it. I enclose a diagram of the small boats.

A few days later, Aufzug and Metzger, the butcher and baker aboard the *America*, came in to say their vessel had just returned from a West Indies cruise.

Aufzug was bubbling with details he wanted radioed to Hamburg—all about underground plane hangars which he said the United States was building on St. Thomas, one of the Virgin Islands.

"*Ja*, that's right," echoed Metzger. "We know—because we've just come back from there."

That was one message which the FBI "forgot" to send AOR.

Meanwhile, the Gestapo was sending its payment money through so many agents and using so many channels that Sebold grew dizzy. Lang, the Norden bombsight spy, complained to him one day:

"My friends in Mexico are broke. They say that a courier sent with $1,000 for them skipped away with it. Tell Hamburg."

Sebold mentioned that in a courier message sent by way of the ring's "letter-box" in Brazil; and also the fact that he hadn't received the money he had been told was coming from a man in Mexico.

In reply, AOR radioed:

Your letter via Brazil received. The money situation is not clear. Our Mexican friend should have paid you 300; Dunn 300; Lilly 300. Did you and Dunn receive 300? Don't ask Lilly.

The reason for not asking Lilly Stein was plain. That avaricious female, even if she had gotten the money, would say she hadn't. At any rate, it was plain that the "Mexican friend" had indeed skipped with the money.

Two weeks later, Erich Strunck, the waiter on the *Siboney*, arrived with $500 to be spread among the com-

plaining spies and keep them contented for a while. He
also took time to boast to Sebold how the Nazis were
causing fires in neutral ships—by the use of "incendiary
pencils" placed in the ships' cargoes. These were small
tubes containing chemicals and were self-igniting.

The intrigue continued. For a while, the Gestapo was
excited over a plan to send Duquesne to spy at Dakar,
Africa, and pointed out to Sebold, "Dakar is very important." But Duquesne complained there was no way
for him to leave America without exciting suspicion. So
the plan was dropped.

In return, Duquesne suggested that, for $300, he'd be
glad to steal the secret of a new poison-gas shell being
developed at the DuPont plant, at Wilmington, Delaware.
The money was quickly sent, and Duquesne, always cautious, wrote out a receipt Sebold wanted for evidence
against him in this fashion:

Received 300 pamphlets from H.S.

In the meantime, another member of the spy ring was
introduced to Sebold. This was Leo Waalen, still a German citizen, who worked as a painter at the Wood Yacht
Basin, City Island, the Bronx. Between him and his shipping clerk friend, Rudolph Ebeling, material began pouring into Sebold's office on the latest developments in our
Navy, ranging from torpedo boats to battleships.

Then one day Waalen walked quickly into Sebold's office near Times Square and said, "Please lock the door."

Sebold locked the door to his office. Waalen reached
into his inside pocket and brought out a brown booklet,
which he handed to Sebold.

The latter opened it and read:

A secret document containing confidential information
and must be treated as such. This is the property of the
U. S. Government and should be returned on request.
Anyone finding this document should mail it, with name
and address, to J. Edgar Hoover, Department of Justice,
Washington, D. C.

[86]

Sebold examined it further and discovered it was a secret manual which had been issued to key defense plants. It gave instructions on how to combat sabotage.

"Very interesting," Sebold commented.

Waalen snickered. "Interesting, but also very dangerous—for us. Send it to Germany."

This was one more tidbit the Gestapo didn't get. But Waalen didn't know that. He also didn't know that in the next office to Sebold's was a Special Agent of the FBI, who was pressing himself close to a little hole above the molding, listening to all that was said and writing it down —for use as evidence bolstering Sebold's testimony.

A few days later, Waalen introduced Sebold to another ring member, George Schuh, a carpenter working at Camp Nordlund, the German-American Bund's rendezvous in New Jersey. Schuh had a hot tip—that England's Prime Minister Winston Churchill had arrived secretly in the United States aboard the British battleship *King George*. He wanted the information sent to Germany, so that the ship carrying Churchill could be torpedoed on his way back. Churchill didn't arrive until nearly a year later, but anyway it proved that Schuh was trying.

Waalen was daring enough to attempt anything. One day, he, Metzger and Strunck were in Sebold's office. Strunck mentioned that on his last trip to Lisbon, the agent there, Duarte, had told him how he had bribed a courier working for the British diplomatic service. Every time the courier was given a mail pouch for London, he brought it to Duarte first, so that the contents of the letters could be photostated for Berlin to read.

"There's a British courier from Washington who always travels on my ship, the *Siboney*," he added. "I sure wish I could lay hands on the stuff he's carrying."

"We'll do it," said Waalen. "I'll travel with you on the next trip. We'll take it while he's asleep."

"I've got a better idea," said Metzger. "Because when he awakened, he'd have the ship searched. We ought to grab it, and simply push the guy overboard."

[87]

Sebold decided the plot had gone far enough. "I've got orders from Hamburg," he said, "to keep you guys from violence. It'll just make trouble for all of us."

That ended the matter.

Waalen next showed up with something the Gestapo had been clamoring for—navigation charts of the New England coast and St. Lawrence River.

"I need something," he said. "I'm trying to get the names of munitions ships sailing from New York for England. But the names have been painted over. Tell Hamburg I need $100 for a pair of field glasses so I can figure out what's going on in the harbor."

Sebold sent the message, and the money was quickly forwarded.

Waalen bought the binoculars and got busy with them. One result was that on April 28th, 1941, he told Sebold to inform Germany that the American freighter *Robin Moor* was sailing on May 3rd for an African port. This item wasn't sent over the FBI's radio station.

But on May 21st, the *Robin Moor* was torpedoed and sent to the bottom 600 miles off the Cape Verde Islands. This made it plain to the FBI that it still had much work to do before the case was complete; either Waalen or another spy had sent the information by some other method than the FBI's station.

The free-lance spy Duquesne, in the meantime, was trying to make good his promise to give Germany something on America's poison-gas secrets.

He strolled into Sebold's office on December 22nd, 1940, and handed over some negatives and a written description of a new gas shell.

"I got it at the duPont plant in Wilmington," he boasted. "I sneaked into the plant, spent eight hours inside, and took the pictures. It is something modern and entirely new."

He followed this brazen accomplishment with a cunning letter he sent to the Army's Chemical Warfare Service, at Washington. It was written on the impressive stationery of the "Security Service Company, 60 Wall Tower, New York." He wrote:

We are interested in the possible purchase of a chemical warfare device which may not be original . . . We understand that you publish a pamphlet on the subject for those interested. If this is true, please let us know where and how we can get a copy. For your information, if it has any bearing on the matter, we are American citizens and would not let anything of a confidential matter get out of our hands.

But the clerk at the Chemical Warfare Service, using good sense, turned the letter over to the FBI, and one more item was written down in the damning evidence against Duquesne.

The FBI might have arrested Duquesne without further delay—but to do this before it was ready to round up all the spies at one time was taking too great a risk. To arrest only one or two might cause the others to take fright and flee.

Duquesne was important because of the way he had of sneaking around and using his itchy fingers. And also because he was cunning enough to use other information transmission belts besides Sebold's.

One day, the FBI station got an AOR message asking Duquesne to provide information on a new American baby incendiary bomb. The spy had Sebold radio back that this bomb was nothing new; it was similar "to the one I sent you through Wang in China a couple of months ago, the one containing thermite and phosphorus."

And so it went. Spy Kleiss came in with diagrams showing how the liner *America* had been equipped with guns and turned into a U. S. Army transport. Spy Strunck got into some trouble with the Customs because of bonds he was trying to smuggle to Lisbon, and AOR soon radioed Sebold to have Strunck lie low for a while.

In February, 1941, four months before the American public was informed that its troops were in Iceland to protect our arms shipments to Britain, AOR radioed:

now many U. S. A. airplanes has Great Britain received since outbreak of war? What preparations are being made in Greenland and Iceland for air convoy?

The trans-Atlantic air bulged with all the orders coming from AOR to bribe American aviators, steal bombsights and torpedo secrets, pay $500 to this spy and $100 to that one. Sebold received two $5,000 sums via Mexico, with which to pay the never-satisfied snoopers.

Meanwhile, either through Sebold or through surveillance of men already under suspicion to see whom they were conniving with, the FBI put some more small-fry spies on its list.

There was Gustav Wilhelm Kaercher, a Staten Island Bund leader and utility company draftsman. There was Heinrich Karl Stade, a stocky musician who played the bull fiddle. Then there was a pair who worked together: Max Blank, a clerk at the German "Library of Information" in New York, and Oscar Stabler, a ship's barber on the S. S. *Excambion,* who took Blank's stuff across to Lisbon.

And finally there was another pair who tried to sell Sebold the idea of blowing up President Roosevelt at his Hyde Park home with a package of dynamite—Paul Bante, an iron worker, and Richard Eichenlaub, who ran the Little Casino Restaurant in "Yorkville," New York's German section.

Eleven

But these small-timers didn't interest the FBI as much as the bigger fellows. One of the suspects who began assuming greater importance was Carl Reuper, the machinist who had been assigned by the Gestapo, while he was visiting Germany, to go back to the United States, get an aircraft plant job and betray Uncle Sam.

Sebold had already met him and given him some money sent by Hamburg but Reuper's rôle was still obscure.

Reuper worked in the experimental shop of Air Associates, Inc., at Bendix, New Jersey. One day he stopped at the bench of Walter Nipkin, a draftsman, and said, "I notice you have an accent. Are you German-born, too?"

"Yes," Nipken replied. "But I'm now an American citizen."

"Me, too," Reuper said. He went on to pump Nipken about the latter's attitude toward Hitler, but Nipken was noncommittal.

A few days later, Reuper asked Nipken to come to his home for dinner. It was on that evening that he confided he was a Nazi agent.

"And you can be one, too," he urged. "All those important blueprints going through your hands!"

Nipken remained silent.

"You'll be well paid," the other continued. "And after the war, just like me, you'll be given an estate and have nothing to worry about."

Nipken replied he'd think it over. And on the next day, this loyal American went to the FBI office at Newark to tell his story. And he agreed to cooperate with our spy-fighters in giving Reuper enough rope to hang himself.

Here was a strange coincidence. Nipken and Sebold had been born in the same town in Germany. As kids, they had played together. Yet neither knew the other was in America and neither knew that the other was helping the FBI trap a pack of Nazi plotters.

Before long Nipken and Reuper were thick in "conspiracy." They would meet in their autos on Highway 2, near Bendix, and Nipken would hand over a blueprint of whatever Reuper wanted; once it was of a warplane's hydraulic pump, another time it was of an anti-aircraft gun.

What Nipken didn't mention was that he had got the stuff from Frank Hill, President of Air Associates, and that the drawings were of obsolete models. And when he brought Reuper picture negatives which the latter demanded, Nipken didn't mention that they had been purposely blurred by FBI cameramen.

But Reuper was overjoyed. He took Nipken to his home overlooking the Hudson River and showed him how to use microfilm.

"But don't develop the film until you're ready to give it to me," he warned. "Keep it undeveloped, locked in your car. So if you get into trouble, all you have to do is expose the film—and it's ruined as evidence against you."

But a few weeks later, Nipken received a scolding.

"You've got to do better," Reuper said. "Germany tells me the films you gave are so fogged that they don't show anything when exposed."

Nipken promised to do better next time. But when he continued turning over stuff which didn't satisfy Hamburg, Reuper thought of another way to make Nipken useful.

"You ought to quit Air Associates," he urged. "And get others to quit, too. If we can get enough to quit, their production will be paralyzed."

Nipken said he'd think it over.

One day, Reuper stopped at Nipkin's bench and his hand rested for a moment on the table. Then he "accidentally" dropped a coughdrop.

"Pick it up," he whispered, "and the note lying beside it on the table."

The note contained a phone number for Nipken to call.

It turned out to be that of Paul Scholz, a book salesman for the Germania Book and Specialty Company across the Hudson in New York City.

But the FBI told Nipken he didn't need to contact Scholz—Agents were already watching him.

He had been seen hanging around with Reuper and with Axel Wheeler-Hill, the wolf-faced spy whom the Gestapo had sent over to run a radio station independently of Sebold.

But there were headaches for a long time. The set wouldn't work; it had to be scrapped and another one built.

In the meantime, Wheeler-Hill had been airmailing or sending by courier the information he and his helpers were picking up. His job, it will be remembered, was to be a tip-off man for Hitler's submarines. He was to prowl around the New York waterfronts, and send word whenever a munitions ship sailed with Lend-Lease supplies for Britain.

The Nazi U-boats would then take care of the rest with their torpedoes.

But finally, in April, 1941, he was able to go on the air with his secret shortwave station. His first message informed Germany of the frequencies he would use, and the times he would send. The second message told of the sailing of the freighter *Indian Prince*, laden with twin-motored fighting planes.

He was often on the air after that, twirling the dials of his equipment on the sixth floor of an apartment house at 563 Cauldwell Avenue, the Bronx. He didn't know that, on the second floor, another man was also twirling dials—a Special Agent of the FBI.

The G-man was there to intercept and make a record of what Wheeler-Hill was sending. But the stuff was obviously in code. The FBI suspected it was the same code which Sebold had been told to use. The only trouble was, this Agent had no way of knowing what key book to use. Sebold had been using *All This And Heaven*

Too. But Wheeler-Hill was using *Half-Way to Horror.*

Between the fact that the FBI wanted to muzzle Wheeler-Hill before he did too much harm and the fact that it considered its case against all of the spies pretty complete, the FBI men began considering the roundup they had long planned.

There was another reason for pouncing on the suspects. Two of the ring's couriers, Paul Fehse and Bertram Zenzinger, had been arrested by other Federal men for having Nazi propaganda in their possession. Even though they pleaded guilty to the charge of failing to register with our State Department as propaganda agents of a foreign power and were sent to prison without much publicity, the FBI feared that the rest of the spies would become panicky and perhaps try to flee.

On top of this, another courier, Rene Mezenen, the ring's steward on the Pan-American Airways plane, "Dixie Clipper," was caught by Customs men and charged with smuggling precious platinum to Portugal.

In Washington, FBI Director Hoover decided that any value in allowing the rest of the gang to incriminate themselves more was outweighed by the risk. He ordered that the case be brought to an end.

Twelve

THERE WAS ONE last thing the FBI decided to do. To bolster its case, it wanted to show the jury what spies looked like in action and to back up the testimony Sebold would be called on to give.

This was to be done by motion pictures. So FBI cameramen began operating. One day, the Gestapo radio station sent over one of spymaster Nikolaus' latest brainstorms. He had heard that the Norden Company, manufacturers of the famous secret bombsight, kept its address out of the New York telephone directory. He wanted Lang, the gang's Norden spy, to supply the address.

That was a good excuse with which to summon Lang to Sebold's office near Times Square.

The sad-faced traitor came and allowed himself to be led again into a recital of how he had taken the bombsight's secrets to Germany "in my head."

But in the next room, with his ear close to a hole in the wall which was invisible to anybody in Sebold's room, sat a Special Agent taking down all of the incriminating conversation.

When Sebold told Lang about AOR's latest request, Lang snorted and said the Gestapo was crazy. He went over to a telephone book, ran his finger down a page and pointed triumphantly to the listing for the Norden Company.

And through another hole—up above the molding—another G-man was putting all this on the turning film of his little movie camera. Spy Waalen was caught in the same camera trap a few days later.

Soon afterward, another FBI cameraman did the same thing in a different way. Slipping in and out of doorways along upper Broadway, he had his humming camera follow Sebold, Metzger and Aufzug as they strolled along in earnest plotting talk.

But the best and most important movie of all came

on June 25th when the cunning free-lance Duquesne walked into the trap.

On June 23rd, he had sent Sebold a note, saying he would call on the 25th with much important information. In another envelope he sent something he wanted rushed to Germany immediately. It contained a sketch and an explanatory letter written on U. S. Army stationery:

Description of the new Rocket Grenade Gun. This gun throws rockets, hand grenades and incendiary bombs to a height of 1,500 feet with great rapidity. Parachute attached to it is made of pliofilm, a transparent rubber for flares. The guiding fins are folded inside the barrel—open when the projectile begins its flight. The gun also fires an anti-tank grenade of about 20 ounces. The gun has a slotted base which fits over a groove that may be clamped to any solid body to ease the recoil.

He had signed the report with the signature he was now using: a rubber stamp which left the imprint of a green cat.

The "cat's-paw" seal was also on another item in the envelope—a photograph of the latest-type U. S. Navy "mosquito fleet" speedboat.

So the eagerness of the FBI to learn what else Duquesne had up his sleeve is understandable.

The spy came with a full load of stuff, producing sketches and photos and describing what they meant: a new gas-mask diaphragm; an all-purpose shell; an airplane that could carry a tank beneath it; a new big tank he had just seen while sneaking around at the Army's maneuvers in Tennessee; something else he had seen on the Tennessee trip—an anti-tank device. It was a one-man pillbox buried in the ground. When the tank passed over, the man inside the pillbox sent a shell into its vitals.

All this and much more Duquesne explained, throwing out his arms to explain the size of a weapon, picking at his nose, ruffling his hair, lighting one cigarette from another. And seven feet away, in the other room, it all went down in a Special Agent's notebook and on an FBI camera.

"You've got to be careful carrying dangerous stuff," Duquesne advised Sebold. Then he pulled up his trousers leg to show how he carried papers inside his sock.

Sebold was listening to all this patiently, and munching on some caramels, unwrapping one, popping it into his mouth, then unwrapping another—trying to keep his eyes from the camera peephole and taking good care not to "steal the scene" from the main performer.

The spy gestured at Sebold's candy. "Did you know you could make an incendiary bomb easy?"

"How?" asked Sebold, stopping chewing for a moment.

"Take one of those candies, break it in two . . . *(the details he described have been deleted in the public interest)*. But you can make a better one from chewing gum. I've used that method in the past. You chew the gum thoroughly, then you . . . *(the details have been deleted for the same reason)*. You see, it's handy because it won't explode until the temperature reaches 75 degrees. But I personally prefer the ordinary bomb you make from a piece of lead pipe. By the way, have you got some slow-burning fuses?"

"Why?"

"I was hanging around the General Electric plant up at Schenectady some time ago. I think I know how I can blow the place up."

Sebold said he wasn't outfitted with fuses. He promised to send Duquesne's stuff across to Germany and the spy departed.

FBI men chuckled when the moving picture film was developed. Sebold had done his "planting" job perfectly. He had kept Duquesne on the "hot seat," a chair placed where the spy was always in view of the camera, right below a clock whose hands wrote mute testimony to the fact that Duquesne spent nearly two hours there. A wall calendar showed the day of the month. Every time Duquesne handed a photo or sketch to Sebold, the lat-

[97]

ter would pretend to examine it, holding it up so that the movie camera could scan it.

Now the case was complete. FBI Director Hoover marshaled his forces. His terse orders went out—a simultaneous roundup of the entire lot.

Squads of Special Agents had been keeping the spies under surveillance and knew exactly where to pick them up. On the night of June 28th, 1941, swift raids took place simultaneously. The G-men's trap closed with lightning speed.

Duquesne was found at home in his New York apartment examining a "blackout lamp" which his itchy fingers had picked up somewhere. His mistress and courier, Evelyn Lewis, was there, too, clad only in a smock, working on a sculpturing design. But the FBI men were in no mood to enjoy blissful domestic scenes, and took the protesting couple along. Lang was caught out at a Long Island tourist camp. The other prize spy, Heine, was taken at his home in Pleasant Ridge, Michigan. Some of the couriers who happened to be traveling were arrested out at sea.

And with the spies were taken their radio equipment, their cameras, typewriters and other paraphernalia. And also plenty of incriminating evidence of other kinds—Wheeler-Hill's code book, letters the spies had carelessly neglected to destroy, notes, etc.

Even the wily ones had been careless. In Heine's home was found a card on which was scrawled, "L.S.—127,54" and also "E.E.—LMP."

FBI puzzlers, thanks to information they already had, were able to make Heine admit these referred to Lilly Stein, 127 54th Street," and "Ernesto Eilers, Lima, Peru," two of Heine's "letter-boxes" to whom his German bosses had told him to send his reports.

In Duquesne's flat was found a letter the spy had just written to spymaster Nikolaus, explaining that some important material which he had mailed by way of the ring's agent in China had been intercepted by the British.

When Scholz was nabbed, he tried to tear up a small piece of paper. But an Agent grabbed it in time. On it was a message written in German which the spy had prepared to send:

S. S. *Miramar*, 12,000 tons, with airplanes for Trinidad, Suez Canal, left yesterday morning. Pacific fleet again back to Pac. Ocean.

A piece of paper in Reuper's home puzzled the searchers for a while until one of the Agents solved the problem.

On the paper was written *Stinfragler* and *Fehdoldse*. When an Agent asked, "Don't those mean the names of three of your pals—Franz Stigler, Fehse and Dold?" the spy shrugged and jeered, "Pretty good, aren't you? You don't expect me to say yes, do you?"

When the news of the arrests became public, the FBI knew it might as well dismantle its Long Island radio station. But it still kept calling Station AOR over in Germany to see what message the Gestapo might now care to send.

But the Gestapo swallowed its tongue. It didn't go on the air with anything. Hitler's supposedly shrewd and highly efficient secret police had been outwitted and fooled as no other secret service in world history had ever been. From May, 1940, until June, 1941—that is, for thirteen months—it had been in communication 501 times with agents of the FBI; had poured out its innermost secrets to them. Every day of these thirteen months the Federal Bureau of Investigation had made fools of the Gestapo.

Meanwhile, the Nazi spies were giving their statements to the FBI men. Some of the small fry admitted they were guilty. So did the Sperry Gyroscope spy Roeder, who thought he'd get off with an easier sentence that way. Some, like Lang, wept and said that they had been unwilling dupes of the Gestapo. Some, like cunning Heine, claimed that they had been collecting only industrial information. Duquesne asserted he was only an inventor interested in the latest industrial gadgets—and defied the FBI to prove him a liar. He, like the others, didn't yet know that Sebold had been working for Uncle Sam all the time.

The entire lot were indicted by a Brooklyn Federal Grand Jury on July 15th—thirty-three prisoners in all. Every one was indicted on a count of spying for Germany, and most of them on another charge of failing to register as agents of a foreign government.

The German government itself was named as a co-conspirator, and many of its agents out of the FBI's reach, like spymaster Nikolaus over in Hamburg, and the "letter-boxes" scattered all over the world, were also named, in order to better prove the case against the thirty-three who had been trapped.

Of these, only Heine—the one-time $30,000-a-year man—had the wherewithal to supply $25,000 bail. Ironically enough, he furnished it in bonds of the Government he had been trying to overthrow—the United States.

The rest went to jail to await their trial. But even long-time crooks wanted nothing to do with spies. The spy ring's three women members were heckled and jeered so much at the Women's House of Detention that it became necessary to serve them their meals in their cells, rather than risk their being beaten up by other women inmates.

By the day the trial opened, September 3rd, seventeen of the prisoners had pleaded guilty. Some of them were even willing to testify for the Government in hopes of reducing their own sentences. But sixteen others, including the "Big Three,"—Lang, Duquesne and Heine—decided to fight it out.

With so many defendants involved, and so much intrigue that had been going on for three years, even the lawyers sometimes got all mixed up in their dates and names. But there was one man who always was ready to straighten them out—a keen-faced, gray-haired man with black robe who sat below the American flag, Federal Judge Mortimer W. Byers. And he was very human in his actions, too. One day, the Court clerk stood up and whispered to him that the Brooklyn Dodgers had just won a World Series game. The Judge's face broke out into a broad grin. Then he returned to the serious business at hand.

It was plenty serious. The United States Government had not been caught napping. It had rounded up the same treacherous types that, over in France and Norway, had betrayed those tragic nations to the Nazis.

But instead of going to the firing squad, the prisoners were facing a fair trial, with every chance to explain their actions away. As Waalen had remarked to Sebold upon news of Fehse's arrest:

"He's lucky he wasn't caught like that in Germany. Over there, his head would no longer rest on his shoulders."

The prisoners were fortunate in one thing. America wasn't yet at war. If she had been, they would have been facing the war-time penalty for espionage—death. As it was, they were facing only prison terms.

They met the situation, each according to his own character. Wheeler-Hill acted as if it were all a big joke. Lang's sad face was longer and paler than usual, and he looked as if he wanted to die. He seemed on the verge of weeping, and he actually did so when on the stand.

Duquesne's bold, dark eyes were continually darting around the courtroom. He seemed to be expecting to see a confederate somewhere in the audience, and Federal Marshals kept their eyes open for any attempt he'd make to duplicate one of his past escapes from custody.

The audience and jury listened with rapt interest when Federal Prosecutor Harold Kennedy outlined the case and told him the FBI had outwitted the Gestapo.

Then he called, "William G. Sebold."

From the back of the courtroom, a broad-shouldered,

poker-faced man ambled up to the witness stand. In measured tones, his eyes steady and unwavering, he told his story. It was a fascinating recital by a man who had escaped out of the grip of the Gestapo—an American citizen who, under terrific pressure, had been loyal to his country; a man who hadn't cowered when the Nazi hatchet men threatened to wreak their vengeance upon him and his relatives still in Germany. He had gone to work for the FBI, convinced the Gestapo that he was willing to be Hitler's spy, and risking his life, had helped bring the Nazi spy ring's elaborate structure down in ruins.

When, some hours later Sebold trudged out of the courtroom, he was closely followed by three men with roving eyes who kept their hands in their gun pockets. They were FBI Special Agents assigned to keep Sebold from any vengeance which the long arm of the Gestapo might be planning. And particularly from any attempt to seal this brave man's accusing lips.

In addition, newspaper photographers were forbidden to take any pictures of him. The FBI didn't want his face to become too familiar to the Nazis.

Sebold returned to the witness stand again and again, each time the Government turned its battery of evidence upon another prisoner.

One hundred radio messages were read, each one involving spy Duquesne, with Sebold sitting on the witness stand explaining what Duquesne was doing to merit so many messages.

Then the founder and director of the FBI's "Questioned Documents" section gave a technical man's view of the subject. He proved that Duquesne's material had been typed on a typewriter found in the spy's flat, that "Jimmy Dunn's" signature matched Duquesne's handwriting, and that the "cat's-paw" seal had been made from a rubber stamp found in the spy's possession.

Other witnesses appeared against the arch-spy, including Else Weustenfeld, who admitted that she had been the mistress for five years of Hans Ritter, spy-master Nikolaus' brother, and had brought Duquesne money and instructions.

But the high spot in the evidence against that spy came when the windows of the courtroom were darkened. Additional guards posted themselves around the prisoners to prevent them from escaping. A screen was put up and a moving-picture show began. It was the FBI movie of Duquesne plotting with Sebold. And on the witness stand sat an FBI Agent supplying the dialogue—Duquesne's entire conversation with Sebold while the movie camera was making its record.

As representative of *True Detective*, I attended the long trial, which lasted more than three months. I looked quickly at Duquesne when the lights came back on. His usually supercilious face wore a sickly grin.

Then the Government turned to another bigshot—Heinrich Heine, the auto sales manager who had toured the East pumping information on our aviation industry, even sneaking data from his own relatives. But Heine's chickens had come home to roost. Up to the witness stand, one after another, marched eleven witnesses who told of his scheming. One of them was Gordon Spittel, the son of Heine's wife's sister. The youth related how Heine had fooled him into giving information about the Martin Bomber plant where Gordon had worked.

When the Government next turned to Herman Lang, the Norden bombsight spy, it produced just enough evidence to cement its case. Defense attorneys tried to prod Sebold into telling more about the secret bombsight. Judge Byers interrupted:

"I'm not going to permit any further questions along that line. I deem it harmful to the interests of the United States to permit any closer inquiry on that subject."

And when the statement which Lang had made concerning the bombsight to the FBI after his arrest was introduced into court by the Prosecutor, Judge Byers read it first. Then he said:

[103]

"In the interests of national security I am going to physically cut out portions of this statement before it is shown to the defense."

Whereupon, producing a pair of scissors, he snipped two questions and answers from the statement. In this way, he prevented publication of bombsight information which could have helped Germany's Nazis.

The defense tried to prove that Lang had never, in his job as a Norden inspector, seen a complete Norden bombsight. Whereupon, the Government called Erhard Bierbach, vice president of the Norden company, to the stand. And he testified that Lang's job had included the inspection of completed bombsights.

But all questions of how the bombsight works were ruled out by the court.

The Government finally rested its case, and it was now up to the defense. The prisoners began parading to the witness stand with their stories ranging from "I didn't know I was doing harm" to "Sebold made me do it." At one time, court recessed for ten minutes to allow Lang to complete his weeping spell.

Duquesne tried every wile at his command. He blandly denied ever having seen any of the other prisoners before in his life. He claimed that whatever he had done was against Britain, not the United States. He tried to scoff at Sebold's testimony but his attempts fell flat.

He waved his hands to emphasize his truthfulness and ogled the women in the jurybox.

He admitted that he had been sharing an apartment with Evelyn Lewis, when the Prosecutor asked about circumstances of his arrest.

"But you were preparing to marry her, were you not?" defense attorney Walsh asked.

"Yes, I was about to marry her when we were arrested."

Judge Byers leaned forward and asked, "How long had you been preparing for marriage by sharing an apartment?"

Duquesne had to admit, "Eight months."

The spy tried every trick in his repertoire. Sometimes he cooed. Sometimes he yelled so loudly at Prosecutor Kennedy that Judge Byers had to warn him against contempt of court.

In explaining his aliases, he said:

"Well, I was a fugitive from a bughouse. I did it to hide my identity as an ex-lunatic."

But even this change of pace—an obvious attempt to make his actions seem those of a mentally ill man—failed to convince anybody. The FBI had gone deeply into this adventurer's past life. He admitted that he had lied about his birthplace in a W. P. A. job application, that he had lied about having a dependent, that he had lied in claiming to be a major in the World War and in parading as a graduate of Oxford University.

Before the trial ended, two of the spies, Stade and Kleiss, became discouraged when they heard the evidence against them, and pleaded guilty.

Prosecutor Kennedy summed up his case with the plea to the jury to find all of the defendants guilty of belonging to "an intelligence service which had a gun pointed at our head, waiting to let it go off."

Immediately afterward, he asked that the $25,000 bail on Heine be revoked. Through furnishing the bond, Heine had been able to remain at liberty. At noon, when the other prisoners were being led back to the pen, he would walk out of the courtroom with his lawyer, as though they were the best of friends going out to have lunch. The Government didn't want Heine at liberty—ready to flee—in case he was found guilty.

The case went to the jury on December 12th, more than two months after it started. December 12th was five days after Pearl Harbor; it was one day after Germany and Italy declared war on the United States.

Judge Byers referred to this in his charge to the jury:

"About twenty-four hours ago, the incident which had

(Continued on page 108)

NAME OF SPY, WITH PROFESSED OCCUPATION	SENTENCE RECEIVED	
1. Frederick J. Duquesne *Professional spy*	18 years;	$2,000 fine
2. Herman Lang *Bombsight inspector*	18 years	
3. Edmund Carl Heine *Auto sales manager*	18 years;	$5,000 fine
4. Everett Minster Roeder *Gyroscope plant engineer*	16 years	
5. Carl Alfred Reuper *Airplane plant machinist*	16 years	
6. Paul Al. W. Scholz *Book salesman*	16 years	
7. Franz Joseph Stigler *Ship's baker*	16 years	
8. Paul Otto Fehse *Ship's cook*	15 years	
9. Axel Wheeler-Hill *Trolley conductor*	15 years	
10. Leo Waalen *Painter*	12 years	
11. Lilly Barbara Carola Stein *Artist's model*	10 years	
12. Erich Strunck *Ship's steward*	10 years	
13. Conradin Dold *Ship's chief steward*	10 years	
14. Erwin Wilhelm Siegler *Ship's butcher*	10 years	
15. Heinrich Clausing *Ship's cook*	8 years	
16. Richard Hartwig Kleiss *Ship's chief cook*	8 years	
17. Rene Emanuel Mezenen *Clipper plane steward*	8 years	

NAME OF SPY, WITH PROFESSED OCCUPATION	SENTENCE RECEIVED	
18. Bertram W. Zenzinger *Seaman*	8 years	
19. Else Weustenfeld *Stenographer*	5 years	
20. Alfred Brokhoff *Ship's mechanic*	5 years	
21. Rudolph Ebeling *Shipping clerk*	5 years;	$1,000 fine
22. Heinrich Carl Eilers *Ship's library steward*	5 years;	$1,000 fine
23. Josef August Klein *Commercial photographer*	5 years	
24. Oscar Richard Stabler *Ship's barber*	5 years	
25. Adolf Walischewski *Ship's steward*	5 years	
26. Gustav Wilhelm Kaercher *Draftsman*	22 months; $2,000 fine	
27. Felix Jahnke *Soda clerk*	20 months; $1,000 fine	
28. Paul Bante *Iron worker*	18 months; $1,000 fine	
29. Max Blank *Bookkeeper-clerk*	18 months; $1,000 fine	
30. Richard Eichenlaub *Cafe proprietor*	18 months; $1,000 fine	
31. George G. Schuh *Carpenter*	18 months; $1,000 fine	
32. Heinrich Carl Stade *Bull fiddle player*	15 months; $1,000 fine	
33. Evelyn Clayton Lewis *Sculptor and playwright*	1 year and 1 day	

been forecast eventuated. It would be sheer affectation if we tried to ignore it. It is unfortunate that this development should have taken place. In my opinion, the duration of the trial has been very considerably prolonged, and unnecessarily so, by the strategy on the part of some counsel for the defense. I hope you will be able to disregard it entirely.

"Bear in mind," he pointed out, "that men are not sent to jail in this country for their opinions. A man is entitled to believe that the German race is a superior race, and that the world was created in order that the German race might dominate it. As long as he does nothing to the detriment of the United States, there is no attempt on our part to discipline him merely for what he thinks . . . Consider the evidence carefully. If you are not familiar with it after these three months, there is nothing I can add to help you."

But the jury decided that the prisoners had been guilty of much more than mere thinking. It found every one guilty of espionage.

"You have rendered a very substantial contribution to the welfare of the country which you and I hold very dear," Judge Byers told the jury when he dismissed them.

Heine, the wealthiest of the lot, said he would appeal the verdict. Thirteen others later filed notices of appeal: Lang, Dold, Walischewski, Stigler, Reuper, Scholz, Eberling, Eilers, Duquesne, Klein, Wheeler-Hill, Waalen and Strunck.

The entire batch of thirty-three—those who had pleaded guilty and those who had been found guilty—came up for sentencing on January 2nd.

The first man to face his punishment was Herman Lang, the Norden bombsight spy.

His lawyer pleaded for clemency.

"He of all men knew the value of the Norden bombsight," Judge Byers replied slowly and gravely. "He of all men knew to what use it might be put by the 'chivalrous' powers of the Axis in waging their war against civilization." He turned to Lang, "I sentence you to serve two years on the first count and eighteen years on the second count, these terms to run concurrently."

Lang looked as if he were going to weep again when two deputy marshals led him away to the prisoners' pen.

When Duquesne stepped forward, Prosecutor Kennedy described him as "a bold and unscrupulous liar."

To which Judge Byers replied, "I find no mitigating circumstances in this man's case. I shall not indulge in expressing my own opinion. My views might be less temperate."

The usually voluble Duquesne said nothing when he heard himself sentenced to eighteen years, but later, as he was being led down the corridor, he let out a loud jeer, "Long Live America!"

Heine also netted an eighteen-year prison term for himself, in addition to a $5,000 fine.

The attorney for Roeder, the Sperry Gyroscope spy, argued that his client deserved leniency because his guilty plea had saved the Government money.

Judge Byers retorted, "He did not choose to gamble on the verdict of a jury." Roeder got a sixteen-year sentence. The same sentences were handed out to Reuper, Scholz and Stigler, the courier who had been going under the name of Aufzug.

It took two hours and a half to sentence the long parade of spies. Two of them were brought in from Atlanta Penitentiary, where they were already serving short terms. These were Fehse and Zenzinger, the couriers. Fehse now got fifteen years more, and Zenzinger got eight years. The rest got sentences proportionate to their importance and guilt in the spy network.

This was the most important spy round-up in world history and to the FBI goes the credit. The record stands as it is shown here on pages 106 and 107.

NOTE—*A fictitious name has been given to the man referred to as "Ernst Bohm" in this story.*

The Mistake of Agent X

NOTE: Addition of this story by Albert E. Brager to those by William Gilman completes the picture of the insidious methods of German espionage.

HERBERT KARL FRIEDRICH BAHR was born in the small town of Klosterfelde, Germany, and came to the United States, accompanied by his mother and brother, George, when he was thirteen years old. His father, Helmuth R. Bahr, a frugal and industrious laborer, had preceded the little family by six months, settling in Buffalo, New York. Dark days had come upon their native Germany, which was on the brink of chaos, and this made them appreciate all the more the bounties which their adopted country had begun to bestow upon them.

June 5th, 1933, was a proud day in the elder Bahr's life, for it was then that he stood with upraised hand and, tense with emotion, uttered the pledge that made him a citizen of the United States. Automatically, that act of his father's bestowed upon Herbert, who was in his nineteenth year, the privileges of American citizenship.

The youthful Bahr was particularly blessed in the land of his adoption. He had grown up into a husky lad with a mind that was alert and keen. Attending the Buffalo Technical High School, he graduated in less than the customary four years and made his sports letter eight times. He topped his classmates in scholastic standing, being selected valedictorian, and received the Dartmouth Alumni award for all-around leadership, character, and achievement. Finally, his outstanding attainments resulted in his receiving a free scholarship to Rensselaer Polytechnic Institute at Troy, New York.

Tragedy had in the meantime struck the Bahr family. Shortly before the youth's graduation, his father was killed when a boiler exploded at the plant where he had been employed. Herbert, as a result, wanted to sacrifice his higher education in order to get a job and help support his mother, but she insisted that he should avail himself of the free scholarship and he finally capitulated.

Though it was necessary for Herbert to wait on tables in the dining hall at Rensselaer and do various other chores in order to earn money for necessities not provided in the award, he continued to participate in sports and burn the midnight oil with a vitality that was amazing to his classmates. When graduation day rolled around in June of 1938, he not only received his degree of Bachelor of Mechanical Engineering but also won a coveted prize that was one day, paradoxically enough, to lead to a terrible reckoning.

He had been awarded an American Exchange Student Scholarship by the Institute of International Education of New York City and now, on the morning of October 8th, 1938, was aboard the S. S. *New York* on his way overseas to begin postgraduate study. He was setting out for the Old World to secure his degree of Doctor of Engineering.

Bahr landed at Hamburg ten days after he left New York, proceeding directly to the *Technische Hochschule* in Hanover where he presented his credentials, arranged for a room in a boarding-house, and in due course started his studies.

Not long after this Nazi spies, ostensibly "advisors" in various student organizations, began to show an interest in him. He in turn learned that they were checking on him with a view to determining whether he could be entrusted with special responsibilities and this tickled his vanity. When the Mayor of Hanover included him in an invitation given a student group to travel throughout the Reich and Sudetenland at the expense of the Government, he was not loath to believe that the Nazis were regular guys, and not as they had been pictured back in America.

After the completion of his first year of study, young Bahr availed himself of the opportunities given him to put his talents to practical use, doing drafting work in several factories having government contracts. But so much did he think of his ability that he became a persistent kicker, demanding more money for his services and telling himself that when he returned to America it would not be with an empty pocketbook.

The Nazi agents who had been observing the pompous, self-assured student smiled faintly. Vanity and greed they recognized were the weak spots. It was a case of playing up to these qualities before inserting the opening wedge which would draw him into their expanding web of intrigue.

One day the *vertrauensman*—a liaison agent between the factory and the government—called him aside and told him that if he played his cards well he would one day have an opportunity to make a lot of money.

"But how?" Bahr wanted to know.

"You'll find out in due course," the other replied.

Shortly after Bahr started attending school again, he was summoned to the office of the *Referendar Fur Auslandsdeutsche*, the leader of an organization set up ostensibly to aid those of German birth who had returned to the Reich, but in reality the man worked in close coordination with the Gestapo. That official introduced him upon his arrival to another man who, since his name is unknown, will be called Agent X for the purposes of this narrative. The latter, a dark-haired flabby-cheeked individual of medium build, greeted the student cordially and invited him out to lunch.

When the two were seated in a restaurant some minutes later, Agent X made a few conventional remarks, then launched into a discussion of airplane engines. He wanted to find out how much Bahr knew about such things and other modern devices in plane development.

Bahr admitted that his education along such lines was limited but was quick to add that when he was studying

[112]

in the United States it had been his intention to major in airplane engine design.

"You have the brains to grasp the subject with little difficulty," Agent X replied. "We need some one over in America to furnish us with certain confidential information about new developments in aviation. We have observed you now for some time and know that you're a safe person for us to deal with. You will be doing a great service for the land of your birth and will be well paid at the same time."

"What will I have to do?" Bahr asked eagerly.

Agent X went on to say that the German High Command was not yet quite ready to disclose the details of the scheme. "I can tell you this much, however," he added. "We will arrange to make it appear that you are the bonafide representative of one of our inventors who has given the American manufacturing rights for his patent to the General Electric Company at Schenectady, New York. This will give you access to the right people and no suspicion will come upon you."

Bahr hesitated, but not because he had any scruples about betraying his country. He was weighing the element of danger involved, but reflected finally that espionage, which ought really to be a paying business, was dangerous only if you were fool enough to get caught. He believed himself to be too astute to fall into any trap. Besides, he kept telling himself that the Nazis were masters at perfecting schemes that could outwit the intelligence agents of other nations.

"I'm ready to undertake any mission you may assign me to in the United States," he said finally, "and I promise to do my part well."

In the days that followed he discovered that he was a fair-haired boy both at school and in its subsidiary, the Institute for Steam Engines, where he began making drawings of steam turbines for the government. He found out that he could come and go as he pleased, sleeping late and taking time off for his own pleasures, without a word of reproach from anyone. He was paid well and was not docked for absences.

Months flew by, during which he continued to live this charmed existence. The professor at the *Technische Hochschule* assigned to him an easy topic for a thesis with which to obtain his degree of Doctor of Engineering. This was a design for a steam turbine unit which consisted merely of reaction blading and he started work on it with the feeling that it was like taking candy from a child. In the meantime, Agent X had called upon him again to advise him that plans for his departure were maturing.

Early in October, 1941, he received another summons from the *Referendar Fur Auslandsdeutsche*. Upon his arrival in that official's office he found two men from the Gestapo awaiting him. One of them, a heavy-set man who spoke English fluently and who appeared to be about forty years old, was named Karl Bauer. The other, tall and several years younger, went by the name of Dr. Otto Baum.

"Things are coming to a head," Bauer said. "We have been assigned to give you instructions regarding your pending mission to America."

Bahr nodded, but wanted to know what had happened to Agent X, the man who had first broached the subject to him. Bauer explained that this individual had been transferred temporarily to another district.

The Gestapo men continued to play their cards with caution. They told Bahr that in due course of time he would be advised of the specific tasks which lay ahead and that their present purpose was chiefly to have him meet the German inventor who held the patents on the machine manufactured in America by the General Electric Company. It was essential, they explained, to make him familiar with the details of this invention so that he would be able to discuss them intelligently and thus raise no suspicion in the United States that his real business was something entirely different.

The two men escorted the eager student to a waiting automobile. When the three seated themselves in the tonneau, the chauffeur started the car and in a few moments it was rolling along a country highway. After more than an hour's ride, the driver turned off the main road and entered the town of Kassel where he brought the automobile to a halt in front of a pretentious residence.

Bahr followed the Gestapo agents into the house where he was introduced to a man named Max Buchholz, a bespectacled, middle-aged individual with a prominent Adam's apple. After several hours during which the inventor went into detail about his patent rights and the relationships existing between himself and the American concern, the three visitors left. Bauer and Baum were convinced that Bahr had assimilated sufficient knowledge to make his pose as the Buchholz representative appear genuine.

Things began to take more definite shape in the weeks that followed. The Doctor of Engineering degree was conferred upon Bahr in November, much earlier than was customary. At about the same time he went to the United States Embassy in Berlin, upon instructions of his Gestapo tutors, to get his passport revalidated, the allotted time for his stay having expired.

Toward the end of the month he received a wire from Bauer requesting that he come to the Kaiserhof Hotel in Munster. When he arrived there, he found that the hostelry was infested with Nazi agents. The Gestapo agents, Bauer and Baum, met him in the lobby and escorted him to a suite that had been reserved.

"Now down to the real business we go," Bauer said, rubbing his hands together with evident satisfaction. He opened a portfolio from which he extracted two loose-leaf note books. "What the Reich wants you to find out when you get back to America is down in black and white in one of these books. This other one, the *Handbuch Der Luftfahrt*, is a reference book concerning

[115]

the organization and technicalities of aeronautics in all nations and meets the practical needs of every pilot. This will also come in handy to you in pointing out the type of information we want."

Baum opened one of the brochures to a mimeographed page and set it on a table in front of Bahr whose eyes glanced hurriedly through the contents. He read:

1. What is the composition of the latest type of bullet-proof glass?
2. Information on armor plate constructed of rubber and steel.
3. Latest developments in the construction of navigation instruments for aviation and of aeroplane engines (is it true that an engine of 3000 horsepower is being built and where?)
4. What is the largest caliber cannon that is being used in planes? (succession of shots, how ammunition is stored, how fed to gun?)
5. Where are aeroplane engines tested? (how big are the plants, the number of employees, the number of planes put out, where are the bottlenecks?)

For the next hour or two, the Nazi agents went over these details verbally with Bahr, enlarging upon each point and then, much in the manner of college professors, asking him questions to see if their instruction was being absorbed.

Bahr remained in Munster for the following three days, during which time the two Gestapo agents continued to coach him on the mechanism of airplanes, supplementing these teachings with sketches to illustrate the various principles they discussed. He took to this naturally and his tutors were delighted with his progress. He returned to Hanover with assurances from them that the time for action was fast approaching and that he would receive final instructions from them in the near future.

Several days later, however, he was surprised to receive a letter from Bauer, who stated that it had been decided to go no further with the scheme to have him represent the inventor, Max Buchholz, in America but that he had another way in mind which would still get him to the United States. The real purpose remained the same, the only difference being that another method would have to be employed.

This message was conveyed to him on November 30th, 1941, seven days before the Japs attacked Pearl Harbor —which was most significant. No reason was given for this sudden change in plans, nor did Bahr question it. In the light of what was to happen later, however, the only reasonable explanation seems to be that the German High Command had advance knowledge of the Japanese program. War with the United States would obviously nullify that part of the plot wherein Bahr could pose as an accredited commercial agent.

Less than a month after American might had arisen to avenge the foul blow of Japan, the two Gestapo men once more summoned Bahr to the Kaiserhof Hotel in Munster. The latter, after exchanging pleasantries, wanted to know under what plan he would now make the trip to the United States.

"You're going to escape from the Reich," Baum replied with a thin smile.

Bahr frowned and looked worried.

"You're really not going to escape," the Gestapo agent said reassuringly. "We're going to make it look as if you did. Your passport will be stamped with various dates by the Gestapo, to imply that you were under surveillance, just like we do with real Americans. Then you'll dash across the Swiss border and we'll shoot at you to make the whole business seem true. You can tell your story in Switzerland and, being an American citizen, the United States Embassy will undoubtedly help you get passage across."

Bahr, after thinking this over, told the two Nazis he thought the scheme was a good one. Then he frowned. "There will be investigations and what-not. It will take time and money," he said. "What explanation will I be able to give for having in my possession a sizable sum? Students, you know, are usually broke. It may cause suspicion."

"We've thought of everything," Bauer replied smugly. "Here, read this and I'll explain."

The Nazi agent handed the young man a typewritten résumé of the history of a Jewish family that had come into the clutches of the Gestapo. The traitor did not flick a facial muscle as he read the summary which traced the life of a man named Richard Damann who had been head of the Social Democratic party in the province of Hann-Braunschweig. He had been arrested by the Gestapo and was now doomed to be beheaded. His wife had only recently been sent to a concentration camp. Her "offense" had been that she had sold several of her husband's stamp collections to raise money with which to flee from persecution.

"What's all this got to do with my trip?" Bahr inquired when he finished reading the summary.

Bauer then explained that they wanted him to familiarize himself with every detail of the Damann family life so that he could build up a plausible story as to how he came by the money which would later be given him. He could, for example, pose as a friend of Mrs. Damann who, just before her arrest, had turned the proceeds of her stamp collection sales over to him for safe-keeping. Better still, he could even say that he had secured the funds through the sale of plans for a steam turbine to the doomed man. And Damann, Bauer remarked, would not live long enough to deny it.

"But such stories are likely to be spiked when Mrs. Damann is released," Bahr protested, "or if there are any other living relatives."

"Have no fear on that score," Bauer replied with an impatient frown. "We have investigated everything about the family and know that the Jew's relatives are dead. One of Damann's brothers left Germany some time ago for Cape Town in South Africa where he died, while a nephew who had been living in New York is also deceased. There were no children and, so far as Mrs. Damann is concerned, I can promise you that she will not come out of the concentration camp alive."

"This is a master stroke," Baum interposed. "Your alleged consorting with Jews will make it appear that you are opposed to the Nazi cause and for this reason the Gestapo was on your heels. Help along that impression when you get across. Mingle with Jews over there and keep away from anyone whom you know to be sympathetic to the Reich. No one will suspect you then."

The two Gestapo agents spent the rest of the afternoon giving Bahr further instructions. He was urged not only to secure information about aviation devices but also told to get a job in an aviation plant so as to obtain samples of bullet-proof glass, armor plate, and other pertinent material.

"Just hold on to whatever samples you may be able to get," Bauer told him. "We will let you know in due course how these things are to be brought out of the United States."

Three names and addresses to be used as "mail drops" were also given him with instructions that he was to commit them to memory. These were Otto Lindt, Bahnhofstr. 74, Zurich, Switzerland; Don Julian Rubio-Chaule, Viriato 71, Madrid, Spain; and Alfredo Ney, Capacabana St. Travesse, Leocardia 19, Rio de Janeiro, Brazil.

Baum then extracted two fluffy bits of cotton, each about thumb size, from an envelope. "These contain a chemical that will convert water into invisible ink," he said. "All you have to do is simply to drop one of these cotton pieces into eighty cubic centimeters of ordinary faucet water. You must use a good quality paper which has a minimum of wood pulp. The pen to be used is merely a small swab of cotton on the end of a toothpick. You'll have to block your letters to keep them from overlapping on the sides and blurring. Use this ink only on one side of the paper and let it dry. Then, on the other side, you will write in ordinary ink an innocent letter in language that no one will suspect."

More meetings with Bauer and Baum followed during the next few days. Finally, on February 18th, they decided that their espionage pupil was ready for his "graduation." That afternoon Agent X, whom Bahr had not seen throughout the intervening months, put in an unexpected appearance at the suite in the Kaiserhof Hotel. Bauer and Baum took their leave, saying that their work was finished. It now became evident to Bahr that Agent X, who had originally broached the subject of the conspiracy to him was one high up in Gestapo circles.

The two left Munster that evening, riding in an automobile to Dortmund where they stayed in an inconspicuous hotel overnight. Here Agent X produced a bundle of currency and explained that the Gestapo had decided to give him $7000 in American funds as well as 500 Swiss francs for use in the neighboring country. Two thousand dollars of the United States money was in $100 bill denominations, the balance in $50 greenbacks.

"This money," the Gestapo agent said, "should be quite sufficient for a while. Three thousand dollars of it is for yourself, two thousand more, we figure, should cover all expenses on the trip over, another thousand should be sufficient for initial traveling expenses in America and the remaining thousand you might use to bribe or loosen up the tongue of anyone who is in a position to give you valuable information."

Bahr nodded, assuring the Nazi official that the financial arrangements were quite agreeable. The latter finally produced a needle and thread, ripped the seams of the lining of Bahr's overcoat and the jacket of his brown suit, and began sewing a major portion of the money into the clothes. He withheld $1200 which he handed to Bahr who pocketed it for current use. One of the chemically treated cotton balls was also sewn into the padding of Bahr's suit coat while the other was tucked under the lining near the latch of his gladstone bag.

The following morning the two men left for the town of Sekingen, which is directly on the Swiss border. Here Agent X pointed out the bridge that led into Switzerland and gave him explicit instructions about the manner of crossing it. Then the Gestapo agent got out of the car, walked over to the near-by customs office and held a brief conversation with the officials there.

"Everything is all set," he announced when he returned to the automobile.

A half-hour later, Bahr, with suitcase in hand, walked to the bridge approach. Though the sentry paid no attention to him, he waited until his back was turned and then made a wild dash across. When he was more than half-way over, two rifle shots came whizzing by him from the German side, but he kept right on going.

The Swiss guard ordered him to halt as he came panting across the bridge. He was placed under arrest and taken to the Swiss customs office where he explained that he was an American citizen who had run afoul of the Gestapo and emphatically demanded that his plight be called to the attention of the United States Consulate.

The "escapee" was turned over to the Swiss military police who began an immediate investigation. Their search revealed nothing more than the comparatively small sum of money in his wallet, an American passport dated at frequent intervals by Gestapo stamps, and an assortment of wearing apparel such as might be the property of an ordinary traveler.

Though Bahr's story had the ring of truth to the Swiss officials, there was something decidedly strange about it in the eyes of attachés at the American Consulate whose attention was called to the case. Their inquiry revealed that he was a citizen of the United States but they could not swallow the fantastic tale of his professed experiences in Germany.

However, they did not disclose their suspicions to him. Instead, they made him the subject of a confidential report to the State Department in Washington, which in turn called it to the attention of J. Edgar Hoover. Little did Bahr know that FBI eyes were now upon him.

After going through the various formalities necessary under the laws of Switzerland when one has entered the country illegally, he was finally released. He took a room with a family in the town of Aarau and began looking around for means of transportation back to the United States. The quickest way to return, he knew, was on the *Atlantic Clipper* but when he tried to book passage he learned that, because of previous reservations, he could not hope to fly on it until late in August. Other means of travel were also difficult to obtain and indirect routes through other countries were fraught with danger because of the possible inquisitive interest of officials.

He had in the meantime written to Bauer through the mail drop in Zurich, explaining his predicament and the consequent delay in securing passage. Bauer replied through an additional camouflaged address, that of FM. C. J. Saridaki, Galata, Bereket, Can. 9-10, Istanbul, Turkey, that he had faith that Bahr would find a way to solve his difficulties.

Weeks flew by, during which the young man was wrestling with his problem. Finally, in mid-April, he received a mimeographed announcement from the American Express Company in Zurich where he had applied for information about passage to the United States that the *Drottningholm*, the diplomatic exchange ship, might also take non-official passengers if there was room. The prospect of sailing on this vessel which was scheduled to leave from Lisbon, Portugal, buoyed up his spirits.

After going through the necessary formalities, he took a train for the Portuguese metropolis, arriving there early in May. He secured a room at the Hotel Europe and went to see the American Consulate the following

[122]

morning about the possibility of securing a berth on the *Drottningholm*, but his hope of immediate departure received a shock when he was informed that President Roosevelt had just issued a directive making it a violation of Federal law for anyone to bring more than $250 in American currency into the United States without making a declaration of it. He also learned that there was insufficient space for him on the first trip of the vessel, but that he could reserve accommodation for its second trip.

Additional letters passed between Bahr and Bauer in the days that followed. Still another name and address of a mail drop was sent to the American spy. This time it was Ivante Wennberg, Banergatan 5, Stockholm, Sweden, who, he was advised, was to be considered as a classmate in the school at Hanover for the purposes of correspondence. But in none of the missives to him did the Gestapo agent make any suggestion as to how he could circumvent the American financial regulations, except to state vaguely that a way could surely be found.

On the day before the *Drottningholm's* scheduled departure from Lisbon, Bahr received a request to come to the offices of the American Consulate.

"There's been a cancellation," the Vice-Consul informed him when he arrived, "and we find that you may get passage on the first trip after all."

Bahr was now in a dilemma. Much as he wanted to get to the United States as quickly as possible, he was uncertain what course to adopt regarding the money in his possession. He could of course declare it and, if any questions were asked regarding its origin, fall back on his supposed acquaintanceship with the Damann couple for a plausible explanation. But there was an element of risk here and he decided against taking a hasty course. Time, perhaps, would point out a better way, so he made some vague excuse to the Vice-Consul about not wanting to sail on the initial trip of the liner. That official wondered why the man who had been so persistent in his attempts to secure early passage should suddenly prefer to delay his departure.

The funds in Bahr's possession began to seem like a millstone around his neck. The safest procedure, he decided, would be to get rid of as much money as possible before the time for his embarkation. He reasoned that the Nazis would somehow or other get more funds to him, once he was safely across and under no suspicion.

It began to be a race against time in the spending spree which followed. He started to frequent the Casino of Estoril, the little Riviera of Portugal, which had become the rendezvous of the fashionable world fleeing from Hitler tyranny. He dropped sums nightly at the roulette tables, indulged in vintage wines, and purchased clothes and an expensive camera which he thought he could convert into cash again when he returned to the United States. But, in order not to attract suspicion to himself, he studiously avoided the Café Chiado in the Rue Garetta, headquarters of German agents in Lisbon.

Despite his gambling and high manner of living, Bahr still had left about 1200 Portuguese escudos and $1800 in American currency when the *Drottningholm*, which had in the meantime made the round trip to the United States, was getting ready for its second diplomatic exchange voyage. The longer he pondered on what to do with this money, the more he leaned toward the conclusion that he ought to chance smuggling most of it into the country.

His mind was finally made up. That afternoon he went to a money exchange office where he converted $1500 worth of his notes into two bills the denominations of which were $1000 and $500. On the way back to his hotel room he purchased a box of cigars which he needed for the scheme that was in his mind. He took one final fling at high living that evening and dropped off to sleep, convinced that he had found a way to outwit the United States Customs officials.

Ten days later, on the morning of June 30th, 1942, the S.S. *Drottningholm* docked at a pier in Jersey City, across the Hudson from New York. Four Special Agents of the FBI, whose interest in Bahr had been aroused by the confidential American consular dispatch from Switzerland, were on hand to question him. Present, also, was Customs Inspector John R. Carey to see that Uncle Sam's customs laws were not violated.

The group took Bahr in tow as soon as he walked down the gangplank. Speaking low and deliberately, he showed no signs of fear when the officials began interrogating him in regard to his experiences in Germany. He went into great detail, telling them that he had met a Jew named Richard Damann in a Berlin café where, after a series of later conferences, Damann had bought from him designs for a steam turbine, paying him sums aggregating a total of $7000. As a result of these transactions, he declared, he got in trouble with the Gestapo, and then graphically described his "escape" across the border.

"Don't hand us any bunk like that," Customs Inspector Carey said quietly. "Since when has Hitler allowed Jews to be hanging around Berlin cafés, conversing with Aryans? You will have to hand us a better one, young man."

There was a challenging note in Bahr's voice as he insisted that his story was the truth. He realized that he could not be held on suspicion alone.

Inspector Carey, warned by the suspect's manner, decided to make a most meticulous examination of his effects. Determined to look into every nook and crevice of his suitcase, he dumped the contents out on the ground.

The two loose-leaf booklets attracted his attention and he put them aside after several glances at the contents. Finally, he came upon a cigar box which contained seven cigars and which rested innocently among Bahr's rumpled and soiled clothes. His keen eyes caught sight of an almost imperceptible bulge under the label that lined the top of the box. After carving this paper away with his knife, he found two American banknotes that had been hidden beneath. One of them was a $1000 bill, and the other one for $500.

The FBI Agents, who had been hovering over the suspect during the customs examination, now closed in on him. Though he paled as he faced them, he still insisted that he had done nothing wrong. He might have been a fool, he declared, for attempting to bring the money into the country without declaring it, but it was nothing more than that.

However, it wasn't long after J. Edgar Hoover's Special Agents began interrogating him at the Hudson County Jail in New Jersey, where he was confined as a Federal prisoner, that the impassive-faced Bahr began to realize that nothing less than the truth, supported by incontrovertible facts, would satisfy the FBI men. For days he clung to his melodramatic story, even though a cotton fluff with chemical ingredients for making invisible ink was found by the FBI agents in the padding of his suit coat, and still another was discovered under the lining of the latch of Bahr's valise.

In the face of the Special Agent's persistence he finally began to weaken, recognizing belatedly that further resistance was futile, for, out of his own words the FBI men had spun a web around him that he could never crawl out of. In this case it was an achievement the details of which cannot be told here. But as in all FBI cases, no force or duress was used nor third degree methods of any sort whatsoever; simply questioning. Bahr signed a thirty-page confession—an eye-opening lesson on Nazi spy methods—the main points of which have been set forth in this narrative.

"How much could I be punished?" he asked when he finally affixed his signature to the statement.

Bahr was duly indicted and held for trial. He now faced death or a maximum of thirty years imprisonment, the statutory penalties for treason in wartime.

FBI Technical Laboratory experts meanwhile had analyzed the two chemically treated pieces of cotton and discovered that not only was it a very effective method of making secret ink, but they also found a way of developing it. Neither the composition of the substance that made the ink nor the method of development can be divulged for obvious reasons—but it can be noted that this was another time when Hitlers' smart Gestapo agents slipped up.

On August 17th, 1942, Bahr went on trial in Newark, New Jersey, before Federal Judge William F. Smith and a jury. Assistant District Attorney Thorn Lord was assigned to prosecute for the Government.

He tried to invent a story that might save him. It was his defense that he never intended to do any of the things the Nazis instructed him to do and that he permitted them to believe he was willing to work for them in order to get back to the United States. But this contention on his part was shattered by the emphasis of Assistant District Attorney Lord on the lag of time between his arrival and his final recital of the true facts. The prisoner, lamely trying to explain away this vital blow to his defense, said that the reason for his delay in coming forward with the truth was because he wanted an opportunity to be alone with the Special Agents because "everywhere, no matter where, there are German agents."

"After signing your statement, did you make a remark to the FBI man who had been interrogating you?' asked Lord under cross-examination.

Bahr hesitated a long time before he replied. Finally he uttered a feeble "Yes."

"What did you say to him?"

"I asked him, 'How much do you think I could be punished?' "

This admission wrecked every vestige of the prisoner's defense. The Assistant District Attorney brought his

[127]

cross-examination to an abrupt close and Bahr left the stand, erect but glassy-eyed. Several times he shook his head vigorously as if to clear it and moistened his tongue with his lips.

One week after the trial commenced, on August 24th, 1942, the jurors filed out of the courtroom to begin their deliberations. Two hours later they returned with a verdict of guilty. Nine days after that Bahr faced Judge Smith for sentence. He was committed to a Federal penitentiary for a term of thirty years, the place of confinement to be designated by United States Attorney General Francis Biddle.

Hitler's Master Spy

J UNE, 1941, WILL loom big in Nazi Germany's history. In that month, Hitler performed his sensational double double-cross, by suddenly attacking Russia. In the same month, the United States ordered all of Germany's Consuls to leave our country. That's a step just short of breaking off diplomatic relations entirely, which in turn is a last step before war.

Our State Department informed Germany:

It has come to the knowledge of this Government that agencies of the German Reich in this country, including German Consular establishments, have been engaged in activities wholly outside the scope of their legitimate duties. These activities have been of an improper and unwarranted character. . . .

In other words, the Federal Bureau of Investigation had turned up evidence linking Germany's diplomatic corps with fomenting espionage, sabotage and class-hatred propaganda on American soil.

In taking this drastic step, Uncle Sam showed that he had learned a lot from the first World War, when German agents—while we were still neutral—made our country a happy hunting ground. In 1941, we were prepared to deal with them; in 1914, we were not.

That is why Franz von Papen was able to earn for himself the title, "Prince of Plotters." He could also be called the Duke of Double-crossers, or Dictator-Maker, in view of how later he was the man who put Hitler into power.

As for himself, he wasn't even "von" Papen at the beginning. You had to have that title—indicating that you belonged to Germany's aristocratic, ruling class—in Kaiser Wilhelm days, in order to get ahead.

Papen got it by marrying into the famous Boch-Galhau family of industrial barons. That was in 1910, when he was an arrogant young cavalry officer in a regiment of Uhlans stationed in Alsace. Like many of his fellow lieutenants, Papen needed money all the time in order to "live like a gentleman."

Some of these young officers went so far as to advertise under fake names for rich brides in the Berlin newspapers, a practice which the Kaiser himself finally had to forbid. But Papen—big-boned, keen-eyed and sporting a daring military mustache—got his money an easier way: by sweeping the wealthy Miss Boch off her feet.

Straightway, he bought himself a regimental title, and as Captain von Papen, began to entertain lavishly in his sumptuous new home at Potsdam. He made friends only with those who could be useful.

And before long, due to the Captain's excellent connections, the Kaiser himself was hearing nice things about the dashing officer who wanted so badly to serve his *Vaterland* in a post where his brains would count. For von Papen had no desire to find himself stationed in front-line trenches when war came.

In 1913 his opportunity came. The post of German Military Attache at Washington became vacant, and he got himself named to fill it. A few weeks later, he reported for duty to his superior in America, German Ambassador Johann von Bernstorff.

The job of a military attache is to keep his home country informed of military developments abroad. He is covered by a "gentleman's agreement" between nations. He is made welcome as long as he keeps his fingers out of spying and subversive activities. We had such an attache in Berlin.

But Germany knew war was coming, and von Papen had instructions to give America plenty to worry about at home. So that the outbreak of war in August, 1914, found him in Mexico, trying to get General Victoriano Huerta to start up a revolution against Carranza.

In answer to telegraphed orders, he hurried back to New York to meet a new arrival from Germany, the astute new Commercial Attache, Dr. Heinrich Albert. Outwardly, the latter was supposed to cultivate trade between Germany and the United States.

Secretly, he brought with him a $150,000,000 slush fund. Part of it was for pro-German propaganda, especially to whip up hatred against England by Americans of German and Irish descent. He would take care of this personally. Part was to buy up priorities on raw materials and munitions, so that they couldn't reach the Allies. He would also take care of this through dummy corporations. Part was for organizing rings of spies and saboteurs with which to defeat not only the Allies but America also if a showdown came between Washington and Berlin. This would be in the hands of Military Attache von Papen, and the Naval Attache, Captain Karl Boy-Ed. They would have a free rein. Albert would pay the bills.

As a result, downtown New York became a nest of intrigue. Boy-Ed had his office in a tall building at 11 Broadway. The Hamburg-American building, where Dr. Albert cooked up most of his schemes, was a long stone's throw to the northward. Von Papen's offices were on the 25th floor of No. 60 Wall Street.

Their agents weren't the only ones in the vicinity, however. Offices of the United States Secret Service were in the Customs House nearby. Also near at hand was the headquarters of the British Intelligence, assigned to give the Germans tit-for-tat.

All this had the makings of plot and counter-plot. In such a situation Captain von Papen was determined to make not only the British gasp at his cleverness, but his own colleagues as well. As for the Americans, he knew what everybody knew—that the war had caught Uncle Sam unprepared, either to fight or to protect himself against intrigue.

And so, although the World War had only just begun

and the United States was neutral, von Papen began
his sinister plotting. This required no courage on his part.
He let others do the actual dirty work and run the risk
of going to the penitentiary or firing squad. And, being
connected directly with the Imperial German Embassy,
he could always claim diplomatic immunity if an accusing finger were pointed at him.

The spymaster plunged at once into his first assignment. There was urgent need for fake passports, especially valuable American ones with which German
spies could get into England and France by posing as
U. S. citizens. They were also needed for Germans crossing the seas—spy ring couriers and German Army officers. Many of the latter had settled in North and South
America, but Germany said they still belonged to the
Reich and should come home to fight. However, England had control of the seas and could take them off
neutral ships as prisoners-of-war. Hence von Papen's
scheme to have them pose as Americans.

He looked around for somebody to do the dirty work
and found such a person one day at the German Club,
in New York City. The man was Hans von Wedell, a
German-born American citizen. He had been a newspaper reporter and now was an attorney—hence, he
had a good "front" and knew New York City well.

Judging others by himself, von Papen was convinced
that anybody could be bought, that everybody had his
price. With some it was money, and with some it was
women. With von Wedell, it was vanity.

In other words, von Papen used con-man methods.
The Kaiser himself, he promised, would hear about von
Wedell—and would pin the Iron Cross medal upon him.
The young lawyer, puffing his chest, agreed to become
a forger.

He was coached, given money, and told to go to work.
He set up an office in Bridge Street. Most of his time
was spent finding men who needed money—sailors and
laborers who would agree to apply for American pass-

ports in their own names. Von Wedell paid from $10 to $25 apiece for such documents.

The rest was simple. American passports in those days weren't as spy-proof as they are today. For a while, the applicant didn't even have to submit his photograph.

To the Bridge Street "passport bureau" came a steady stream of agents and officers sent by von Papen. Like a tailor, von Wedell fitted each one with a passport to match.

When the fake Americans arrived in Germany, their passports were taken up and given to spies assigned to work in Russia. Von Wedell was certainly becoming useful.

And then the British pounced upon a German spy using such a passport. When news came that this spy, Karl Lodi, had been executed, von Wedell decided to lay low for a while. A few days later came word that another of his passport-bearers had been arrested at Gibraltar. Von Wedell's courage vanished entirely. Packing hastily, he took the first boat to Cuba.

His chief assistant had been Carl Ruroede, a senior clerk with a German shipping company operating out of New York. Gallant Captain von Papen, who knew his diplomatic immunity would always protect him, convinced Ruroede there was nothing to fear and appointed him to continue the work.

"Von Wedell was stupid," he explained. "But I can see that a man of your high intelligence will not get into trouble."

Ruroede had no way of knowing that London had tipped off Washington to the existence of a fake passport ring in the United States. And he didn't know that a New York politician had been informed by one of his voters that von Wedell had offered him $20 if he would apply for a passport. So that Agent Albert Adams of the Department of Justice was assigned to look into the matter.

Shabbily dressed and acting the role of a Bowery bum,

he offered to find passport prospects among his floater pals. Ruroede was cautious and put him off.

A few days later, Adams dashed in, jubilantly waving four passports. The moment was a good one—Ruroede badly needed passports for men that von Papen wanted to sail the next day on the Norwegian liner S.S. *Bergensfjord.*

He handled the documents and remarked, "They look perfect."

They ought to have been—the State Department having made them out at the special request of the Justice Department.

"But how about the photographs?" Adams said.

"Just watch me," Ruroede boasted. He pasted the photo of one of von Papen's travelers over the one already on the passport and went to work with a dull-pointed knitting needle.

"When it's dry," he said, "the new photo will bear the imprint of the United States Seal—and Arthur Sachse, of the German Army, will have become Howard Wright, bearer of passport Number 45573."

He didn't know that the man Wright in whose name the passport was issued, was also a Justice Department agent.

There were simultaneous raids the next day. One, upon Ruroede's office, netted the forger and his equipment. The other, upon the *Bergensfjord,* produced Sachse and three fellow German officers.

The latter, claiming they had accepted the passports out of patriotism, were fined $200 each. Ruroede confessed, without implicating von Papen, and went to Atlanta penitentiary for three years.

But von Papen had been implicated nevertheless. A few minutes after Ruroede's arrest, the agents ransacking his office had a visitor who believed they were members of the ring and explained, "von Papen sent me here to get a passport." Whereupon, the visitor, a German Navy captain, produced a card of introduction.

He wasn't arrested, but von Papen's card proved useful—experts declared it had been written with the same typewriter used in typing lists of men needing passports, which had been found in Ruroede's office.

However, American officials wanted no unpleasantness with Germany. They hoped that the case would frighten von Papen and cause him to stop his intrigues.

They were only partly right because the spymaster got others to fake passports, although on a lesser scale.

There was another sequel. In his confession, Ruroede mentioned that von Wedell had returned from Cuba—and was a passenger aboard the *Bergensfjord* at the time it was searched.

So the Department of Justice got busy with the wireless. Three days later, a British patrol boat, in mid-Atlantic, took Rosato Sprio, a "Mexican," off the liner. After grilling, he admitted he was von Wedell.

But Fate had a card to play. That British patrol boat never made port. She struck a German mine and von Wedell went to the bottom with her.

Back in America, meanwhile, the gallant Captain von Papen was mixing intrigue with a little private chiseling. Some of it was on the stock market, where he profited from his inside knowledge of German Army plans. Some of it was in padding his expense accounts.

The latter brought him in conflict with thrifty Dr. Albert, in charge of the money bags. Albert declined to help make von Papen a social lion at Reich expense, and finally refused to pay one of the submitted bills—for a golf club luncheon to which von Papen had invited eleven persons at $19 per plate. His note accompanying the bill stated that the expense was "far more than justified in the results secured," but Albert combed through the luncheon guests and couldn't find one who, by any stretch of the imagination, might have proven useful in German intrigue.

Such annoyances made von Papen scheme all the harder, and soon he was laying grandiose plans for something that would win him the promotion he thought was due him. An invasion of Canada. For this he would organize thousands of German-Americans. In powerful motor-boats, they would speed across the Great Lakes on a chosen night and gain their foothold in the British Dominion by machine-gunning into submission such defenseless cities as Kingston and Toronto. Then he could join them and run the new German colony.

But when he submitted the plan to his superior, Ambassador von Bernstorff, the latter, figuratively speaking, doused it with a bucket of cold water. It would never succeed, he said, and would only result in their all being kicked out of the United States. Sabotage, on the other hand, would be safer—and just as effective in the long run.

Whereupon, von Papen bethought himself of something else—to blow up the Welland Canal, through which Great Lakes traffic had to pass in order to detour Niagara Falls. For that job he got Horst von der Goltz, a German agent who had been spying in the Mexican Army. The latter gathered together three confederates, transported 300 pounds of dynamite to Buffalo and made two airplane reconnoitering trips over the canal.

Then he became suspicious that the U. S. Secret Service was watching him, and returned to New York.

The spymaster was disgusted. "You were recommended to me as a daring and experienced agent. Oh well, maybe I can use you as a courier."

He gave the agent some confidential reports which he didn't care to trust to the mails and furnished him with a fake passport. This got von der Goltz, posing as an American named Bridgeman Taylor, through the British blockade to Berlin. A month later, he started back, carrying instructions to von Papen to get busy crippling America's munitions industry with bombs and labor strikes.

He made the mistake of stopping over in England, where British agents learned his true identity and sent him to prison. He was later freed in exchange for a confession unmasking Germany's espionage methods. Meanwhile, Germany got wind of a plan for Japanese troops to help the Allies in France. So from Alfred Zimmermann, Under-Secretary for Foreign Affairs in Berlin, went a cipher telegram to Ambassador von Bernstorff in Washington:

The transportation of Japanese troops through Canada must be prevented at all costs if necessary by blowing up Canadian railways. It would probably be advisable to employ Irish for this purpose as it is almost impossible for Germans to enter Canada. You should discuss the matter with the Military Attache. The strictest secrecy is indispensable.

A month later, on January 3rd, 1915, Zimmermann sent another:

The General staff is anxious that vigorous measures should be taken to destroy the Canadian Pacific in several places for the purpose of causing a lengthy interruption of traffic. . . . Acquaint the Military Attache with the above and furnish the sums required for the enterprise.

Captain von Papen foamed at the orders. Berlin was getting more stupid every day. Why didn't the brasshats back home give him saboteurs capable of so dangerous a task? Or did they expect that he personally would risk his neck? Oh well, he'd give them something just as good, but less risky.

There was an international bridge which crossed the St. Croix River at Vanceboro, Maine, linking the United States and Canada. American munitions traveled over the Maine Central Railroad as far as the boundary and were picked up on the other side by the Canadian Pacific. Canada was dangerous but it shouldn't be hard to blow up the bridge from the American side.

For the job, he needed a willing puppet. And along came Werner Horn. The latter was a reserve lieutenant in the German Army. The outbreak of war found him raising coffee trees in Guatemala. After months, he finally reached New York, reported to von Papen, and said he wanted passage to Germany.

The spymaster studied the big blond and saw he was sincerely full of zeal to fight for the fatherland. So he broached the matter of blowing up the St. Croix bridge.

Horn balked. As a soldier in uniform, he said, he would gladly risk death. It was no dishonor to become a prisoner-of-war. But there was only ignoble death and dishonor of he were caught as a skulking saboteur.

Von Papen clucked. Of course, of course. That was easy to take care of. All that Horn had to do was to pin on his coat-sleeve cuffs tiny pieces of cloth bearing the German national colors—red, white and black. That would be equivalent to a uniform. Horn believed this brazen lie. Another thing worried him. He'd dynamite the bridge, but wanted no part in the killing of innocent persons.

The Military Attache hid his surprise at such scruples, and had a quick answer. The last train over the bridge every day was at 11 P. M. Then there would be six hours before the next train—more than enough time for the authorities to prevent it from plunging into the river.

So Horn traveled to Vanceboro, rented a hotel room, and on the night of February 2nd—with the mercury 30 degrees below zero—lugged his suitcase full of dynamite down the railroad tracks to the bridge.

One place on the bridge would have been just as effective as any other for the blast, but Horn made up in decency what his chief lacked. The way Horn looked at it, America had done him no harm, but Canada was an enemy country. So he didn't stop until he had passed over to the Canadian side of the bridge.

He planted the dynamite against a girder and was about to light the fuse when he heard a locomotive whistle, then saw its glaring eye approaching from the American side. He slipped over the bridge's side and held on to a girder, with the river racing beneath, until the express had roared past. A few minutes later, another train crossed.

It looked to Horn as if train schedules must have been changed suddenly — he didn't know that von Papen hadn't known when that last train would come through, and hadn't cared.

So, to get the explosion over before another train might approach, Horn cut off nearly the entire length of fuse, which meant the blast would occur in three minutes instead of fifty. He lit it and ran back toward his hotel.

There came a blast which wrecked the Canadian side of the bridge and shook Vanceboro. In shortening the fuse, Horn had cut off his own chances of escape. He was found at the hotel rubbing snow on his frost-bitten fingers.

Upon questioning, he confessed readily enough. It would have gone hard with him had Canada been allowed to extradite him on a sabotage charge. But Uncle Sam preferred to try him instead on the charge of transporting explosives, and he went to Atlanta Penitentiary.

In his confession, although admitting he knew von Papen, he didn't implicate the latter. Proof of the Military Attache's role was uncovered later.

But meanwhile, Horn's fate didn't bother von Papen. He was too busy with other intrigues. Aiming at Canada again, he found a ready recruit in Albert Kaltschmidt, owner of a small Detroit machine shop and secretary of the Deutscherbund there.

Like a phonograph record, Kaltschmidt was soon repeating von Papen's words to his close friends: "We must strike a blow for our dear Fatherland. We should not care anything for America, because we were born in Germany and remain Germans at heart. Besides, America will throw us out of jobs, but there will be fine jobs for us if Germany wins the war."

They plotted to blow up the Port Huron tunnel, and

an armory and factory in Windsor, Ontario, across the river from Detroit. The factory did blow up; the bomb at the armory failed to explode and the gang was arrested before the tunnel could be blasted. As a result, six more of von Papen's puppets went to prison for terms ranging from two years to life imprisonment.

The military attache was getting into full stride now. There were being sent to him skillful agents who didn't have any more scruples than he had, and who at the same time could argue him out of some of his more fantastic schemes. There is not room here to list the almost daily outrages which occurred in the three years that America was still neutral, and finally raised American anger to a fighting pitch. Many of them were tied up with von Papen only after the war was over—showing how carefully he managed to keep his hands hidden.

Nevertheless, as far back as 1915, the American Government was beginning to regard the conniving Captain with suspicion.

But Washington held its hand. It didn't want trouble with Germany. It wasn't prepared for war. And it wasn't even prepared for counter-espionage. We had only a handful of agents in the Department of Justice and the United States Secret Service to get the necessary evidence against the plotters.

An agent was assigned to keep an eye on the Captain. One afternoon, the latter sauntered out of the Ritz-Carlton Hotel and strolled idly toward 42nd Street. It looked like just a walk for fresh air. He turned east a block, then turned again down the ramp into Grand Central Station.

When he reached the waiting-room, he began running, presented his ticket at the train gate, and clambered aboard the Twentieth Century Limited just as it began pulling out. His disappointed shadow sent a wire ahead to Chicago to pick up von Papen's trail there.

The spymaster was followed around Chicago for a

day, then he managed to shake off his shadow. For an entire month, the American authorities were without word of his whereabouts.

It was a month in which von Papen got enough plots going to fill a book, all of them along the Pacific Coast. As usual, he gave the orders and made out the checks. His principal aides, who in turn got others to do the actual work, were three "vons"—German Consul-General Franz von Bopp at San Francisco, and two Vice-Consuls, Wilhelm von Brincken and E. H. von Shack.

Their first plot—to blow up a Canadian Pacific tunnel near Vancouver, British Columbia, turned out to be a dud. The man they hired took their $1,500 and then tried to collect twice by informing Canadian authorities of the scheme. As a result, Washington was asked to keep an eye on von Bopp.

The latter, however, was too busy to lay low. He had commissioned two saboteurs to blow up a barge-load of Du Pont gunpowder tied up in Tacoma harbor. On May 30th, 1915, Tacoma and Seattle were rocked by a mighty explosion—the barge had disappeared in a blinding flash of exploding nitroglycerin.

That success found portly von Bopp neck-deep in still another von Papen assignment. It was a plot that had been cooked up in Berlin—to stage a revolution in India. Von Bopp bought two vessels: the *Annie Larsen,* a small freighter, and the *Maverick,* an oil tanker.

Von Papen bought up 8,000 rifles and 4,000,000 cartridges, and sent the ten carloads of "freight" to San Diego. Here, the arms were secretly loaded aboard the *Annie Larsen,* and she sailed with fake clearance papers for a Mexican port. Her real destination was Socorro, an island in the South Seas, where she was to meet the *Maverick,* which would transfer the arms to the oil tanks and go on to India.

But something delayed the *Maverick's* arrival at the rendezvous. The *Annie Larsen* waited a whole month at Socorro Island, then departed and began wandering over the Pacific, not knowing what to do with her contraband.

Meanwhile, von Papen had his fingers in still another pie. He had learned that there were many Hindu coolies working in Vancouver. They were from a section of India hostile to British rule. Why couldn't he hire them to dynamite railway bridges and tunnels in Canada's Northwest?

He paid an agent $4,000 to buy a ton of dynamite and fifty rifles, equipped with Maxim silencers, to murder any railway guards who interfered. The dynamite was delivered. And then von Papen got scared.

The *Annie Larsen* had put in at Hoquiam, Washington, where American authorities seized her munitions cargo and began investigating. Von Papen feared his role in the Vancouver plot might be exposed, and called it off.

His alarm was premature. It wasn't until 1917 that von Bopp and his ring were put on trial, thanks to evidence secured by American sleuths aided by the British secret service, which had been intercepting telltale cables between Germany and the rebels in India. There was a dramatic scene in the crowded San Francisco courtroom when Ram Singh, one of the Hindu leaders, shot and killed Ram Chandra, whom he suspected of being a traitor. Whereupon U. S. Marshal James Holohan shot the murderer dead.

A guilty verdict was returned against twenty-nine of the defendants, von Bopp included, and they went off to prison. But by that time von Papen was safely out of the country. Another to escape prosecution in that case was his saboteur, Kurt Jahnke, who was to become implicated in the Black Tom munitions explosion and who was recently holding a high post in the Gestapo.

But this is getting ahead of our story. We are still in 1915 and we find the spymaster, after his fright, resuming his outrages against neutral America. In the space of two months, he could boast to Berlin of five explosions at Du Pont munitions plants, two at plants of the Aetna Powder Works, etc.

To be sure, he was being damned openly, especially by pro-Ally American newspapers. They pointed out that he was the logical master-mind behind the plots. The Providence *Journal*, supplied with information by the British secret service, which wanted to arouse the American public against Berlin's conniving, printed proof that von Papen had been getting sabotage orders straight from his home office.

But the spymaster blandly went on. He denied the charges as a pack of lies.

In this attitude he was joined by his confederate, Dr. Albert, who was also under fire, having literally been caught napping. His nap occurred on the afternoon of July 24th, on a New York City elevated train. When he awoke, his black briefcase had disappeared.

He blamed the loss on British agents. In reality, the "borrower" was Frank Burke of the U. S. Secret Service, who turned it over to Secretary of Treasury William McAdoo.

The latter was anxious to expose the machinations of the Commercial Attache without admitting that one of his agents had stolen the bag. So he turned its documents over to the New York *World*. And soon the mortified Herr Doctor was reading exposes of his pet schemes— for propaganda and for tying up key munitions materials.

But he put up a bold front and came out with the usual denial. Sharing von Papen's views, he wrote in a letter to his wife (which was intercepted by the British): ". . . Uncle Sam, a great, strong lout suffering from shriveling of the brain, to whom you ought to talk in high language about fine principles and then deny everything, especially if you are in the wrong."

The open plotting by Germany's diplomats on American soil, their contemptuous disregard for American anger—all this was to be echoed by Hitler's Germany twenty-five years later. With this difference: that in 1940, Uncle Sam was better prepared to nip their schemes in the bud.

There wasn't even an effective Federal espionage law until 1917, so that in 1915 it was local police authorities that did most of the counter-espionage work against Germany's spies. Fortunately for the United States, a brilliant sleuth was watching over New York City's important harbor—Captain Thomas J. Tunney, head of the city police department's Bomb Squad. It was he who ran across the tracks of the next of von Papen's important agents.

This agent was Robert Fay. The outbreak of the war found him an infantry lieutenant and he saw some of the bitterest fighting of the war in the Vosges Mountains.

From their examination of Allied shells, the Germans saw that the best of them were of American manufacture. The problem was: how to prevent those shells from crossing the Atlantic. Lieutenant Fay suggested a way. The German General Staff handed him a neutral passport, $4,000 in American money, and told him to report to von Papen.

He reached New York in April, 1915, and had a long talk with the Military Attache in a private room of the German Club. Von Papen gave his okay to the man— an engineer by profession and a fluent speaker of English —and to the plan.

"But you must not be seen with me any more," he said. "I am being watched too much. Our dealings from now on will be through an intermediary."

To help him manufacture the special bombs he had in mind, Fay got Walter Scholz, a former Lackawanna Railroad engineer, and Paul Daeche, Scholz' fellow member in a German society.

Between them, they put together a new idea in bombs, designed to be fitted to a ship's rudder. Fay bought a powerful motorboat, with which to take the bombs out into New York harbor at night, and fasten them to munitions ships.

Then the doomed ship would leave port. Each turn of its rudder would give another wind to a spring in the bomb's mechanism. Finally, the spring would release a hammer which would strike the bomb's percussion cap —and the ship would blow up with the exploding T.N.T. —of which there was enough to sink the most heavily armored dreadnaught.

But one day, in October, Captain Martin, the French Military Attache, phoned a tip to Captain Tunney—he had heard of a supply of T.N.T. being ordered delivered to a garage in Weehawken, New Jersey, across the Hudson River from New York.

Tunney checked and found that the order had gone through several hands—a suspicious fact in itself—and that its final destination was the Weehawken garage, where it would be picked up by a Robert Fay.

Tunney's agents delivered twenty-five pounds of T.N.T. to Fay. Then the latter was shadowed to see what he had in mind. Detectives saw Fay and Scholz go into the woods near Grantwood, New Jersey, and test the explosive power of the purchase. The pair were seized then and there.

A search of Fay's boarding-house and garage uncovered several parts of the ingenious bombs, plus 25 sticks of dynamite, 450 pounds of explosive potassium chlorate, 400 detonating caps, etc.

Fay made a confession explaining his plan, and was sent to Atlanta for eight years; Scholz getting six years, and Daeche getting four.

A month later, Fay escaped from the penitentiary, using a forged pass. Various German Consulates in the United States helped him with money and he finally got into Mexico. There, he stowed away on a ship bound for Spain, where he was stranded and finally, half starved, surrendered to the American Consul in Malaga—with the result that he went back to Atlanta.

With Fay it was the same old story. American authorities felt certain his master was Captain von Papen, but Fay refused to implicate the attache—until three years later.

Not only that, but Fay had been caught only preparing to commit sabotage. At first, judging from the time of his arrival in this country, he was believed responsible for a series of incidents which had made Captain Tunney haggard from lack of sleep: toward the end of April, 1915, the S.S. *Cressington Court* caught fire at sea; two bombs were found in the cargo of the S.S. *Lord Erne*; a bomb was uncovered in the hold of the S.S. *Devon City*. In May, bombs were found on the S.S. *Bankdale,* the S.S. *Samland* mysteriously burst into flames at sea; and a bomb was found on the S.S. *Anglo-Saxon.*

All these ships had sailed from New York. Little wonder that Tunney was jubilant at catching Fay.

But—two days after the latter's arrest, the S.S. *Rio Lages* mysteriously caught fire at sea. Then the same thing happened on the S.S. *Euterpe,* than on the *Rochambeau,* than the *Ancona* blew up.

Sadly, Tunney had to admit there were still other saboteurs in his bailiwick.

What he didn't know at the time was that he was up against the most effective German saboteur of them all, Captain Franz von Rintelen of the German Navy.

The latter was a pain in von Papen's neck, and a thorn in his side. With a half million dollars to finance his activities, von Rintelen had sneaked over from Berlin on a forged passport, and let von Papen and Dr. Albert know that Berlin wasn't satisfied with the progress they were making. He intimated that the Military Attache was only an egotistical blunderer who had stirred up American resentment against Germany more than anything else.

But all that would be taken care of now, he said at a conference, while von Papen sat biting his mustache. "I'll take care of America's munitions. I'll buy up what I can, and blow up what I can't."

The result was that the two "vons" didn't get along at all. Von Rintelen was a genuine member of the German aristocracy, while von Papen had had to marry a rich girl to get into the upper crust. Von Rintelen had been in America before as representative of German banks and was a member of the New York Yacht Club—its only other German members being the Kaiser and his brother, Prince Heinrich.

New York society, unaware of the dapper aristocrat's secret mission, flocked around him, while von Papen sulked at the German Club wondering how to get rid of the interloper.

But when von Rintelen asked him to recommend a trustworthy chemist, there was nothing for the Military Attache to do but comply.

The result was those ship fires and explosions. Von Rintelen's device was simple—and tremedously effective. It was nothing more than a short piece of pipe, divided into two compartments by a copper disc. Into one section went sulphuric acid. In the other, a mixture of sugar and potassium chlorate. Stevedores were bribed to slip one or two of these "cigars" into a ship's cargo.

The acid began eating through the copper disc. And somewhere out at sea, the acid would reach the other compartment, and there would be a finger of fire.

If the ship blew up, that was fine. If the fire was put out with sea water, the cargo became useless.

After von Rintelen got his ship sabotage going, he went on to other things. Keeping his own hand hidden, he organized a "Labor's National Peace Council," which called for an embargo on munitions shipments to the Allies and led to strikes among munitions-loading stevedores. But when it became known that German money was behind the outfit, America's labor unions declined to join it, and the Council died a natural death.

These two failures gave von Papen his chance. He began complaining to Berlin that von Rintelen had squandered money and produced only anti-German feeling in America. It worked—the saboteur got secret orders recalling him to Germany.

At least, the Germans thought they were secret.

In the old Admiralty Building at London was a room

numbered 40. Only a chosen few were allowed entrance into "40 O.B." Its existence was unknown to Germany —even the British public didn't know of its activities until long after the war.

In this room sat Sir Alfred Ewing, a noted British scientist, frail of body but with an enormous head and piercing eyes. Around him was an organization of mathematicians, linguists and secret ink chemists.

Their job was to unmask the next moves of the enemy. Whenever a British agent laid his hands on a secret German cable message, or intercepted a German wireless message, it was the task of Ewing and his men to crack the code in which the messages had been written. To them also went code books stolen by British spies or found on sunken German ships.

By decoding messages concerning the movements of German warships, they were responsible for such British naval victories as those at Doggerbank and at the Falkland Islands. And it was "40 O.B." that decoded the wireless message ordering von Rintelen's return to Germany.

Consequently British Intelligence officers in New York checked on the saboteur's movements and discovered that he had booked passage, using a Swiss passport in the name of "E. V. Gache," on the Dutch steamer S.S. *Noordam* bound for Rotterdam.

Von Rintelen sailed into the trap. When the *Noordam* put in at Falmouth, England, on her way to Holland, the German was taken off as a prisoner-of-war.

Later, when Captain Tunney's men rounded up the ship sabotage gang von Rintelen had left behind, he was brought back to America and sentenced to Atlanta.

Von Rintelen was caught on August 13th, 1915. A few nights later, there was a pre-sailing party on the roof garden of the Ritz-Carlton in New York. Among those present were the German attaches, von Papen and Boy-Ed, and the Austrian Ambassador, Dr. Constantin Dumba. The man preparing to sail for Holland, from where he would go on to Germany, was James J. Archibald, an

American newspaperman who had turned propagandist and dispatch carrier for Germany through the sea blockade.

Two Czech waiters working for the Allied cause saw to it that they served the party, and kept their ears open. They caught enough scraps of conversation to learn that Archibald was due to sail on the S.S. *Rotterdam* and would be carrying documents for Berlin and Vienna.

On September 1st, when the vessel stopped over at Falmouth, the British removed Archibald and his luggage. They found a wrapped package containing 110 articles—a confidential report by Ambassador Dumba, seventeen reports by the German Embassy at Washington, a report to the General Staff from Captain von Papen, a letter from von Papen to his wife, etc.

England made good use of the stuff in showing the extent of German machinations against America. Photostatic copies were given to the American Embassy and to American newspapers.

The Dumba document outlined a plan for ruining America's munitions production—and thereby making her helpless against Germany in case the two nations went to war—by buying up labor leaders, fomenting strikes and going at sabotage bigger than ever before.

"This will be enormously expensive, but in the end the results will be more than commensurate with the outlay," Dumba stated.

Public opinion is sometimes a strange thing. Both Dumba's report and von Papen's letter to the General Staff damned them as planners of sabotage. But what aroused America's anger even more was a sentence in the Captain's letter to his wife,

. . . . I always say to these idiotic Yankees that they should shut their mouths and, better still, be full of admiration for all that (German) heroism. . . .

This came on top of the arrest of Robert Fay, with its strong indications that he was von Papen's puppet.

So finally, on December 8th, President Woodrow Wilson took what became America's first step toward war. He demanded that Captains von Papen and Boy-Ed get out of the country, or be kicked out. For under their diplomatic immunity, they could not be prosecuted. In his message to Congress on the matter, the President declared:

. . . . A little while ago such a thing would have seemed incredible. Because it was incredible, we made no preparation for it. . . . They have formed plots to destroy property, they have entered into conspiracies against the neutrality of the Government, they have sought to pry into every confidential transaction of the Government. . . .

Von Papen thought it would all blow over, and spent a month traveling over the United States. Newspaper reporters pestered him at every step, demanding an explanation of what he had meant by "idiotic Yankees." He held newspapers in front of his face when pictures were taken and held up a paper on which was printed in German, *"Wir haben nichts zu sagen"* (we have nothing to say).

The German Ambassador complained to Berlin that von Papen was only making an utter ass of himself, and the sooner he left the country the better. So, on December 21st, the Military Attache sailed—to be followed on New Year's Day, 1916, by Boy-Ed.

The British had granted both men a "safe conduct"— a privilege accorded to all diplomatic representatives recalled to their countries in wartime. In such cases, it is usual for the traveler to destroy his secret records, or to leave them behind with a safe person. All of von Papen's associates, from the Ambassador down, had warned him not to take any confidential stuff along. But the amazing Captain knew better! He'd pull off a slick stunt. He'd bring his papers to Germany right under the nose of the stupid British.

But the British weren't so stupid. When his ship

stopped at Falmouth on January 2nd, they went through his luggage.

Von Papen exploded, waving his "safe conduct."

"Ah, yes," grinned Sir Reginald Hall, head of British Naval Intelligence, "but that applies only to your person, not to your baggage. Read it again, and you'll agree with me."

There would be dire consequences, stormed the Captain.

"Tush, tush, man," said Hall. "We're already at war, you know."

The British lived up to their promise. Von Papen was allowed to go on to Berlin. But his papers stayed behind, and England lost no time showing them to Washington.

They exposed von Papen completely. He had even carried along the stubs of his checkbooks, showing that over three million dollars had gone through his hands—in the form of checks to the West Coast saboteurs and munitions runners, to Werner Horn, Robert Fay, Horst von der Goltz, etc.

And it wasn't long afterward that this, plus other incidents, led Uncle Sam to lose his patience entirely and declare war on Germany.

But von Papen had plenty of pull in Berlin. He was raised to the rank of major and even got a decoration. Then he had himself assigned to what he considered a safe berth on the staff of General Liman von Sanders in Palestine.

The only trouble was that Arabs under Lawrence of Arabia, with General Allenby's British cavalry, put the Germans to flight. Von Papen barely escaped capture at Nazareth. In his sumptuous tent were found more compromising documents, including one from Boy-Ed in Berlin which carried the warning, "Destroy immediately in the interests of safety."

And once again, the British were able to learn of German machinations, thanks to von Papen's carelessness with documents.

Germany lost the war and, along with the rest of his Junkers clique, von Papen found it the discreet thing to do, to retire to his estate and wait hopefully for the times to change. Having got rid of the Kaiser, Germany's decent citizens were striving to establish a peaceful Republic. They had no use for a conniver like von Papen who made it only too plain that common people were just scum on the boots of an Army aristocrat like himself.

The 1920's rolled on, and little was heard of several men who had seen service in the World War. It was as if Fate was preparing them for the roles they were to play in World War Number 2.

Winston Churchill, who had been Britain's First Lord of the Admiralty, was writing his memoirs. Franklin Delano Roosevelt, who had been America's Assistant Secretary of the Navy, was winning a personal battle with infantile paralysis. An Austrian house-painter named Adolf Hitler, who had been a German Army corporal, was making hysterical speeches to his gang of hoodlums and crackpots.

And what of our gallant hero? He was conniving as usual, this time against his own country's welfare. Thanks to the connections of his wife's financially powerful family, he built up a private fortune as a "fixer" in notorious business deals between French and German industrialists at the expense of the starving German people.

Along with this he posed as a hero of the World War, and got himself elected president of the *Herrenklub*—"Gentlemen's Club." In its clubrooms, he spread his poisonous arguments—the German Republic was doomed, there had to be a return of the good old days: either rule by the Kaiser or by a military dictatorship.

Then with a few rounds of machine-gun bullets, Germany could be cleared of all its nuisances—Communists, nazis, socialists, liberals, democrats, republicans.

He played his game with his cards close to his chest. Politicians of the Catholic Center Party thought he was on their side. But the man he was really backing was Major-General Kurt von Schleicher, who wanted to be military dictator.

Germany's first President, Friedrich Ebert, died in 1925. Dreading civil war unless his successor was a man all the nation could love and respect, Germany chose its World War idol, Field Marshal Paul von Hindenburg.

He meant well but he was a doddering old man at the age of seventy-eight. It was a question of which clique would use him as a tool. Eventually, von Schleicher won, thanks to von Papen. The latter had wormed his way into the aged President's confidence. He knew enough not to pester the old veteran with problems of state, but instead, to listen for hours at a time to von Hindenburg's rambling reminiscences.

His reward came on July 31st, 1932, when von Hindenburg dismissed honest Chancellor Bruening and gave the post to von Papen. Von Schleicher was Defense Minister at the time. It was understood between von Papen and von Schleicher that the former was to keep the post as a "front" for the latter, until the army was ready to take over.

So the former spymaster now held the second highest office in the Reich. It turned out to be a dizzy height. Although they were spilling each other's blood in an undeclared civil war, German Communists and Nazis shared a mistrust of the Army men, and combined forces to make it almost impossible for von Papen to govern. It was two gangs against a third.

But von Papen could play the same game. He needed no lessons in trickery.

As between the two, he feared the Communists more. He convinced General von Schleicher that it was time for a daring step—to put Hitler's Nazis into power. But just for a little while. Just long enough for the Nazis to exterminate the Reds, and for the country to see what a mess the Nazis were. Then, with the Reds wiped out and the Nazis a failure, to move in and take over.

[153]

Von Schleicher agreed. Whereupon von Papen got busy among his industrial baron friends with the same argument. Finance the Nazis, he told them. Help the Nazis win the coming Reichstag election. Let them wipe out the Red menace for you. Then kick them out. Such men at Fritz Thyssen, Germany's steel king (later to flee for his life from the Nazis), agreed to this dangerous game.

The only trouble was that at the election of November, 1932, instead of gaining, the Nazis lost two million votes. They had only a minority in the Reichstag.

Quick action was needed. Late on the night of January 29th, 1933, von Papen took Hitler with him. They awoke old von Hindenburg from his sleep. While Hitler listened with his feelings masked, von Papen painted a picture of the Reds ready to rise in open revolt. Make Hitler chancellor, he begged.

What Hindenburg's thoughts were we don't know. But we do know he agreed.

Then von Papen got to the President privately and had himself named Vice-Chancellor—so as to keep an eye on the Nazis.

Hitler did an effective job of purging the Communists. But it soon became plain that he was becoming a Frankenstein monster—more powerful than the men who had built him up. He was only too willing to purge anybody who stood in his way.

A united front to curb his power was cooked up. Part of the opposition was led by his old friend, Captain Ernst Roehm, head of the Storm Troopers. Part came from the Army clique. On June 17th, 1934, von Papen delivered a speech openly assailing the Nazis.

But Hitler had known all along that the Army men were planning to use him just as a stepping stone. To this was added "treason" evidence against Roehm, furnished by Gestapo Chief Heinrich Himmler.

Hitler knew he had to beat his foes to the punch. On the night of June 30th he struck. By the time his infamous purge was over, his assassins had wiped out Captain Roehm and his Nazi rebels, General von Scheicher and his wife, and hundreds of others.

President von Hindenburg learned about the massacre in time to save von Papen. So, instead of being purged, the latter was made a prisoner in his own home.

What went on there between the conniver and Hitler's bargainers can only be imagined. The fact is that his life was spared—it could easily have been taken a month later when von Hindenburg died and Hitler became sole dictator. Did von Papen accept Hitler's clemency in exchange for informing on his confederates? Here is the record:

His sponsor, von Schleicher, was murdered. So were his two adjutants, Jung and von Bose. So was his friend, Dr. Erich von Klausener, head of Catholic Action. And the corpse of his secretary, Baron von Kettler, was fished out of a river But von Papen wasn't touched.

Not only that, but a month later, Hitler named him as Ambassador of Austria!

At any rate, it was a mutual bargain between two men to whom personal friendships meant nothing. Each had use for the other. Von Papen got himself a berth in the Nazi machine, with unlimited possibilities for a future if and when Hitler became world dictator. And the dictator got himself the kind of "diplomat" he needed.

His agents had just murdered Austria's Chancellor Engelbert Dollfuss in hopes of thereby making a Nazi province out of Austria. But the Austrians, backed by Italy, had re-established their government.

So Ambassador von Papen arrived under secret orders to "soften up" Austria for Nazi conquest. The assignment was right down his alley. With unlimited funds at his disposal, he set up a Nazi Party. He bribed politicians. He fomented strikes, and class war between workers and employers. To Austria's large Catholic population, he fed propaganda that Hitler was their defender against Russia. To Austria's businessmen and aristocrats he confided that he, personally, didn't like the Nazis either, but it was best to go along with them for the time being—then kick them out.

Mixing wheedling with threats, he got Austria's new Chancellor, Kurt von Schuschnigg, to make one concession after another, in hopes of "appeasing" Hitler. But after each concession, von Papen demanded more.

In March, 1938, his Fifth Column inside Austria joined forces with Hitler's invading army, and Austria was conquered. Leaving the Gestapo to clean up what he had started, von Papen returned to Berlin. There Hitler pinned upon his breast a gold-rimmed membership button in the Nazi Party.

The plotter rested on his laurels a while, then was assigned to "soften up" Rumania. Rumania had the reputation of being the most corrupt country in the world. His task proved an easy one. He set up a Fifth Column, with the Iron Guard as its spearhead, and Germany was later able to take over the country without even using her army.

His next assignment came in April, 1939, when he was sent as Ambassador to Turkey. A month later, Turkey signed her friendship pact with England. This was a blow to von Papen's prestige, and he knew full well that Hitler had no patience with failures.

So he hurried to Berlin and explained that he had not been sent to Turkey in time—that he should be given another chance. Hitler gave it.

Back in Turkey, von Papen tried every trick in his bag. But the Turks are a sturdy people. They deported dozens of his spies and propagandists. They spurned his offer to give them the Suez Canal and Iraq's oil in exchange for their joining Germany against England. They refused to be frightened by moving pictures of what the German Army had done to Poland.

He has made enough blunders in his day to prove that he is no modern Machiavelli or prince of plotters. He is just a tool ready to obey any command by his gangster master. As such, his life is forfeit. Hitler is too much of a double-crosser himself to trust his scheming lieutenant, and won't stand for failure. In a way, it would be too bad if von Papen joins the list of Hitler's purge victims. Many of us would like him to live long enough to write his memoirs.

They ought to be interesting—especially if he wrote the truth. Which is very doubtful.

Jap Spies

First came the spies, then came the preparation, then came the stab.

Remember Pearl Harbor! There is no need to repeat here the details of that cowardly attack by Japan's sly, war-crazed navy at Hawaii.

But behind that stab into Uncle Sam's back was preparation—by a host of spies. Nippon never could have timed and delivered that stroke without first knowing every inlet, every sounding, every inch of the emerald waters of the Pacific around Hawaii. Her two-man submarines knew how to slip past our defenses; her aircraft carriers knew where to poise, and the bombers knew exactly where to go.

We had alert spy-fighters who weren't deceived by Japanese politeness and waged undercover war against her snoopers. They got hold of a Japanese naval manual so up to date that it even showed the latest models of America's "Mosquito" boats. They got a Jap map which diagrammed the way the American fleet was spread out when in battle formation near Hawaii—a map made by spies who watched naval maneuvers. There was plenty of such evidence.

However, our State Department for a long time had hopes of winning back Japan's friendship—or, at least, of getting Japan to postpone warlike action. All that has been changed now. Uncle Sam isn't worrying any more about hurting Japan's feelings, and I can reveal details about Japanese undercover treachery that preceded her "all-out" treachery at Hawaii.

Some of her espionage was of the "old-fashioned" variety. For example, there was the Jap who was a prosperous laundryman at Sitka, Alaska, one of our most important naval ramparts along the Pacific. It wasn't until he died, shortly before the war, that the truth came out—he was a commander of the Japanese Navy, masquerading at Sitka for obvious reasons.

And there were times when the Japs could find a traitor American to play ball with them.

Fortunately, America has had but few such renegades. And that's why the Jap spy chiefs had to figure out other ways of getting information. They were badly handicapped. In general, the Jap makes a poor spy. He can be spotted too easily. It's possible for a German Nazi or an Italian Fascist to pose as a loyal American. But a Jap's appearance gives him away immediately. His only chance is to pose as a Chinese. In that masquerade, he can be pretty successful—even Chinese can be deceived.

I remember, one day in New York, running into my old friend, Chen Han-seng, with whom I had spent many pleasant hours in China when I was a newspaperman there. We went to a Chinese restaurant. While we were busy with our rice bowls, I noticed a displeased expression come over Chen's usually mild, scholarly face.

"The nerve of that Jap coming in here!" he said, nodding in the direction of a man who was entering the restaurant.

"I wish you could tell me, Chen," I said, "just how to tell the difference between a Chinese and a Japanese, when they're both dressed in American clothes."

"It's difficult," he nodded. "Even we Chinese find it hard to distinguish. But I can recognize a Jap every time —by the little, shuffling steps he takes. The face can be deceiving. I always look at the feet."

It isn't known just when it was that Nippon's spy chiefs hit upon one solution for their big need—learning how to penetrate America's sea defenses.

But as far back as 1935, the United States Treasury Department began getting warnings of what the Japs were up to, and began passing its tips along to the Navy's Intelligence service. The Treasury was in a good position to learn such things, because among its operatives are sleuths of the Customs Bureau, Coast Guard and Narcotics Division. It's the job of these operatives to keep an eye on what's going on in the sea-lanes and along our waterfronts.

One of the first to smell something fishy—but not just because of the fish involved—was Customs Agent Gwinn, stationed at Los Angeles (he is now a Lieutenant-Commander in the Navy).

"I've been doing a lot of talking lately," he said one day to Customs Agent William Whitney, "to these Japanese fishermen who work out of here. Their boats are always hanging around during our fleet maneuvers. Most of them are aliens—they're still citizens of Japan. What's more, a good many of them aren't just fishermen. Among them are sailors, and even officers, of the Jap Navy."

One top of that came a report from Customs Agent Roy Fisher up at San Francisco. He, too, had become curious as to what was going on. And his keen eyes noted something among members of the "Abalone Fleet"—hundreds of fishing boats, mostly operated by Japanese, which concentrated on catching the abalone, a giant shell-fish.

"I have observed," he reported, "that many of the fishermen wear trousers and caps like those worn by soldiers in the Japanese army. One can easily see clean spots on the caps—indicating where the army insignia has been torn off."

Then, actual incidents began occurring, which bolstered the suspicions. One day, the Customs learned that one of the abalone boats had been seen contacting an out-going Japanese freighter. Then another of the abalone boats got in the habit of wandering away from the rest of the fishing fleet off the coast of Monterey, remaining absent each time long enough to justify the suspicion that it was having a rendezvous with a ship farther out, in the lane where Japan-bound steamers passed. But there were only suspicions. Some of the Jap fishermen made unexplainable trips to Japan. One night, a Jap was seen flashing his car's headlights in some sort of code signal out to sea from Point Pinos, near Monterey.

But in all these affairs, when the Treasury agents did any questioning of the Japs, they ran into a stone wall of very polite shrugging.

Nor were the Japanese fishermen confined only to the California coast. They ranged all along Uncle Sam's Pacific defense area—from Alaska in the north to the Galapagos Islands off the coast of South America. The Japanese Navy had found itself a system of eyes and ears that was working perfectly.

It didn't need to look for Fifth Column supporters among the Japanese-Americans who were citizens of the United States. It could rely upon plenty of Japanese citizens, aliens whom hospitable and friendly Uncle Sam was allowing to flourish in his waters and coastal cities. There were 40,000 of these alien Japs in the Western states of Washington, Oregon and California. There were 37,000 more in Hawaii. Together with Japanese-American citizens, they comprised a third of Hawaii's population.

It was in the ranks of these alien Japanese fishermen that the spies were.

Some of America's guardians were more alert to the danger than others. This was particularly true of men stationed out in the midst of the Japanese intrigue. One was J. Walter Doyle, Collector of Customs at Honolulu. Some of his friends called him an alarmist. But he didn't care. He knew he was on the right track.

Late in 1938, he made a full report to the Naval Intelligence. The picture he drew was not a very pleasant one. One of Hawaii's leading industries was fishing. Ninety per cent of the thousands of sampams in the fishing fleets were run by Japanese, most of them unable to speak English, but thoroughly acquainted with every coral reef that could shelter Japanese submarines, every possible mine field and every possible landing harbor and airfield in the Hawaiian Islands.

He pointed out that many of the Japanese were members, and even officers, in the Japanese Navy Reserve. Their boats were constantly hanging around during U. S. Navy maneuvers. They were equipped with the finest of photographic equipment, with radio receivers and transmitters able to communicate 5,000 miles, with high-powered field-glasses, and with plenty more equipment that didn't help catch fish.

At the same time, he realized how hard it would be to convict any of the Japs as spies. The kind of evidence needed in court was lacking. It was practically impossible to get such evidence. The Japs stuck together like a clan; they wouldn't inform on one another. And a native American, a white man, couldn't get in with them and unearth their secrets—they wouldn't trust anybody but one of their own race. So there were pretty hopeless prospects of getting proof that their frequent trips back to Japan for "medical treatment" or to visit Japan's mineral baths were in reality to give espionage reports, and that their complete sets of hydrographic charts of the Hawaiian waters were for the eyes of the Jap Navy.

But if they couldn't be convicted, there was a way—Doyle decided—in which their fangs might be drawn. He had run across something surprising. Many of the Japs had no legal right to be fishing out of Hawaii.

This was due to an American navigation law dating back to the year 1793. It requires that all vessels of American registry must be owned by American citizens. Such boats pay for a license given by the Department of Commerce, allowing them to operate.

This applies to boats weighing five net tons or more. But for boats under that weight, there is no such regulation. All such fishing boats require is a number, given them free of charge. They can be owned either by a citizen or alien.

What Doyle strongly suspected was that many of Hawaii's fishing sampans owned by Japanese aliens were operating with "small-boat" numbers when, in reality, they were big enough to require American ownership and a license.

The fraud was brazen. One of the sampans that had come to Doyle's attention weighed, he estimated, at least 150 tons net—and yet it was operating with a "small boat" number, thereby escaping citizenship regulations.

The fact is that Uncle Sam had been lenient. The average fisherman's wages were so small and the long hard weeks at sea so distasteful, that few Americans would engage in the fisheries. The United States needed these fish which were in the waters along our coasts. The Department of Commerce broadly interpreted the law regarding vessels that can be numbered and owned by aliens, and the fisheries became a large and important business on the West Coast and in Hawaii. But while Americans ran the canneries and sold the products, Japanese went out and caught the fish.

Doyle got a go-ahead signal from the Treasury and, in March, 1939, started a check-up on Hawaii's fishing fleet. He had only a small staff and there were hundreds of boats that had to be weighed and measured.

The checkup lasted a year. And out of ninety of the boats Doyle suspected, seventy-five turned out to weigh over five tons, although they had been fishing without "big boat" licenses. *And every one of the seventy-five was owned by Japanese aliens.*

As each case arose, the owner was forbidden to let the boat go out fishing any more until it had a proper license. And as each such owner came to the Honolulu Customs House to get such a license, he was shown the regulations requiring that he be an American citizen.

But something strange happened. Many of the Japanese boat owners weren't at all disappointed. They simply pulled out American citizenship papers, and papers proving they were owners of the vessels.

[163]

It was plain enough what had happened. There had been transfers of ownership. Japanese aliens had sold their boats to Japanese who were American citizens.

Collector Doyle's nostrils told him that there was something plenty smelly here. The documents in themselves were genuine enough. But Doyle strongly suspected that many of the new "owners" were simply dummies; and that the boats were still owned by the aliens.

But to prove this would be no simple matter. And that is when the Customs called for help—it called upon Elmer L. Irey's famous Intelligence Unit of the Treasury's Bureau of Internal Revenue. Irey's men were skilled in prowling through books and records. With pencil and paper, they had sent Chicago's gang king, Al Capone, to the penitentiary for income tax evasion when no other law agency had been able to convict him. In like fashion, they had convicted Kansas City's corrupt political boss, Tom Pendergast—and scores of other gangsters, politicians and con-men.

So now, in conjunction with the Customs, they went out to Honolulu to satisfy their curiosity as to who really owned some of those Japanese fishing boats.

They first looked into the matter of the *Tenjin Maru,* an oil-screw vessel which had been found to weigh twenty-two tons. She was an *ahi* boat. In the Hawaiian fishing fleet are two types—the *aku* boats, which go out for the aku, a type of tuna fish, and the *ahi* boats, like the *Tenjin Maru,* which brought back other varieties of fish.

Practically all of these boats are under contract to Honolulu fishing companies, which handle their financial affairs and sell their catch for a 10 per cent commission.

This boat carried License No. 11, its owner being listed as Katsuki Tsumura, an American citizen living in Honolulu.

He was summoned to the Customs House. Yes, he swore in a statement, he was the vessel's sole owner; he had bought her for $2,000 from an American citizen,

[164]

Akiyoshi Shigei, paying for her with $500 of his own money and borrowing the rest from the Pacific Fishing Company, which sold his fish for him.

Whereupon Customs Agent Whitney and Internal Revenue Agent H. C. Parrott went to the office of the fishing company and began going through the books. It was a tedious process of prowling among checkbooks, account ledgers and receipts, but when they were through, they had their evidence—Tsumura was just a dummy owner. The real boss of the ship was an alien named Kinshiro Kimura.

They summoned Tsumura to the Customs House again and threw their accusation of fraud into his face.

"Yes, yes," he said fearfully. "I am not the owner. I have never owned even a share in it. Kimura is the real owner. I did not buy the boat from Shigei, who used to own the boat in partnership with Kimura. That was a lie. Now, please let me go."

The agents looked up Kimura, who turned out to be a slippery Japanese citizen with dislike for everything American written all over his face. But when he heard of the evidence against him, he shrugged and told the story.

He had owned the boat in partnership with Shigei. When he heard that the citizenship regulations were going to be enforced, he had sold his share to Shigei, and then had turned around, secretly, and bought the entire boat back from Shigei for $2,000.

That left Shigei on the ship's papers as "Owner."

But Kimura wanted to be absolutely beyond suspicion. He and Shigei had been joint owners of the vessel; he was afraid that the authorities would suspect that he was still a "silent" partner. So he had the false owner Shigei "sell" the *Tenjin Maru* to the false owner Tsumura.

Each case the Treasury agents looked into was similar to the others, but with a little difference due to circumstances.

When they came to the case of the *Fuji Maru,* an eighteen-ton *ahi* boat engaged in mackerel fishing, they found that it was no longer owned by plump, suspicious Mitsuyoshi Wada, who was always taking trips back to Japan to visit his "sick father."

"Fat Man" Wada, as he was known by Hawaii's Japanese community, had the good luck to be married to a Japanese-American—a citizen of the United States. So with him, the solution had been simple.

In March, 1939, he had "sold" the boat to his wife Sawayo, "for $1 and other considerations"—in the language of the bill of sale, and on the same day, she had taken out a citizen's license for the vessel, No. 13.

The financial affairs of the *Fuji Maru* were also handled by the Pacific Fishing Company, and the Treasury Agents went there to see the books. They found that all accounts were still listed in the name of Wada.

"That is because," the company's manager, Matsuichi Yamashiro, explained, "Mr. Wada is acting as agent for his wife."

The agents learned that some of the provisions for the *Fuji Maru* were sold by Shichimon Abisuzaki, who ran a store at 1221 Ward Street, Honolulu. They went there, and learned that "Fat Man" Wada had just paid two bills, one for $116 and another for $170.

And at another store on Ala Moana Road, they found he had paid a $180 bill. At this store, the proprietor, Mankichi Soranka, said, "Certainly, he is the owner of the boat—although I've heard some talk about his claiming that his wife owns it."

The same evidence against Wada came from a boat builder, to whom the fat Japanese had just paid $850 for ship repairs.

Learning that he was under suspicion, Wada decided to scurry back to Japan, fearful of what the American authorities might ask him about espionage activities. He sold the boat. It was a genuine sale this time, to Japanese-American brothers who paid $4,000 for it.

But the sale provided the clinching evidence against Wada. Treasury Agents heard that details of the sale had been handled by the Pacific Fishing Company. They visited the company office and its cashier, Yuen Poy, showed them the package containing $4,000. Written on the package was, "M. Wada." In other words, the money had gone to the husband, not the wife.

When the investigation ended in March, 1941, it resulted in the seizure by Uncle Sam of nineteen of the fishing boats, heavy fines upon the persons involved, and deportation of most of the guilty aliens.

The American authorities breathed a sigh of relief. But they knew that they had solved only part of the problem, and even that part had been solved pretty late. How much did the Japanese Navy already know?

And then there was the matter of boats under five tons. There was no law forbidding Japanese aliens to own and run such boats, which couldn't go out as far to sea as the bigger ones, but could do plenty of spying off the Hawaii coast. In August, 1941—four months before Japan's attack—Honolulu's Collector of Customs reported to Washington that, although larger fishing vessels were no longer operated by Japanese aliens, there were 231 alien-owned fishing boats under five tons working out of Honolulu—every one of them owned by a Japanese citizen.

And the same situation held true all along the California coast.

In fact, the California Fish and Game Commission put out new regulations shortly before the Japanese attack, aimed at her fishing boat spies. The new law required all applicants for fishing licenses to submit their photographs and fingerprints, and automatically revoked the license of any such boat that operated too near the California coast or came within 500 yards of an American warship.

But all this did not affect the long-distance Japanese fishing vessels which could operate out of Japanese ports and defy all American regulations—ships big enough to prowl all over the Pacific. They could lay mines off Mexico, pick up spy reports off California, and patrol off Alaska in weather too bad for Jap observation planes to operate. A few days before the war broke out, I saw a confidential list of sixteen such ships, one of them big enough to be mother-ship to eight trawlers. After war was declared, several such ships were seized by us in our waters.

The attack at Pearl Harbor proved how much the Japanese Navy knew where it was going, how to get there through our defenses, and what it would find. Before that attack, our defenders could only guess at how much Japanese spies had learned. After that attack, they knew. Kindly Uncle Sam had allowed the Japanese fishermen to earn a living in our waters; and they had repaid the kindness with treachery.

Spying is always a dirty business, and it is one of America's proud claims that we have never used spies, except in wartime for self-defense.

Other countries have descended to the practice of using spies in peacetime, Japan and Germany being the big examples. But there has probably never been any nation that descended as low as Japan did—when she actually used a vicious criminal gang on our West Coast to give her a spy network.

In Japan, the Nipponese look upon the Mikado as the axis of life—here and hereafter. And on our West Coast, the hundred thousand men and women from the Land of the Rising Sun over ten years looked upon an ape-faced, uncouth, unlettered runt of a man as the Mikado's representative on these shores.

His name is Kanekichi Yamamoto. For a decade, he ruled the Japanese colonies in the United States and Canada—aliens and American-born alike. Japanese diplomats kow-towed in his presence and mothers hushed their children by the mention of his name. Cities and states brought him before the bar of justice charged with fourteen separate crimes, including murder, but he never could be convicted.

There was always a catspaw to take the rap for Yamamoto, or an important witness who couldn't be found—alive.

Although nothing more than a brazen hoodlum, he was cunning enough to know the value of having the Japanese Government on his side. He and his henchmen became a clearing house for spy information along the West Coast. As a result Tokyo looked on him as a fair-haired boy. Nothing was too good for Kanekichi Yamamoto. Japanese diplomats addressed him as "Sir," and not just "Mr." When they traveled with him, they looked after the baggage and details—Yamamoto couldn't be bothered.

And before the Federal authorities began looking on him with a sour and searching eye, Yamamoto found it very easy to get along with the American law. In nearly every big police department on the West Coast, he secretly had men on his payroll.

And yet—back in 1924, this little son of Nippon whom Treasury agents were later to call "Little Caesar," was just a fugitive alien, working as a common laborer on the railroads, in lumber and fishing camps of the West Coast. He knew hardly a word of English, and spoke only an uneducated dialect of Japanese. He had few friends and little money. He had come to America during the World War years with an Oriental crew which delivered a Japanese ship to the docks at Seattle. When the crew went back to Japan, Yamamoto took French leave. He stayed in America and began a game of hide-and-seek with American Immigration authorities.

How was he able to rise to such power later? Simply by taking what he wanted.

He rose among the Japanese, in the same way—but not so politely—as the Japanese nation was muscling its way into power. There is a verse which describes this process:

How courteous is the Japanese,
He always says, "Excuse it, please."
He climbs into his neighbor's garden,
And smiles, and says, "I beg your pardon."

He bows and grins a friendly grin—
And calls his hungry family in.
He grins and bows a friendly bow—
"So sorry, this my garden now."

That was the secret of Yamamoto's success, except that
he wasn't always so polite. He first came to the attention of his countrymen in this nation at a Jap gaming
den at Helper, Utah. The game was Japanese fan-tan,
played with pellets and shell instead of cards, as the
Chinese version is often played.

The houseman had just rolled and capped his pellets.
The players were placing their bets on numerals indicating the number they believed to be under the cover.

At that moment, the houseman felt a sharp poke in
his ribs. He looked beneath the fold of his coat and be-
held the business end of a .45 automatic pointed at a
right angle to his belt.

Holding the gun was an ape-faced little Jap—our
friend Yamamoto.

What they said to each other can easily be guessed by
the fact that a moment later, Yamamoto placed his entire
fortune, $200, on a number—and won.

We find him soon afterwards running a string of "slave
markets"—employment agencies for Northwest canneries seeking cheap Oriental help. After that he opened
his first gambling den, the "Toyo Club," in Seattle. It
was soon the nucleus of eight such "clubs" Yamamoto
controlled on the West Coast. And with the help of his
gunmen—led by Hiroshi Ichikawa, an officer in the
Japanese Army Reserve!—he collected his "take" from
a dozen other such clubs.

Along about this time, Yamamoto wanted a wife of
his own race, in addition to the white mistress he was

keeping. He got his wife through the same method of persuasion he had used in the fan-tan game at Helper. He liked the looks of sixteen-year-old Sadako Nakatano, who had been born and raised in Seattle. He didn't bother to ask Sadako what she thought about it. He went to her mother and ordered that a family conference be held. When all the Nakatanos were gathered, Yamamoto began toying with his automatic, and remarked:

"Your pretty Sadako suits me. I want the wedding to be in a week."

The Nakatanos, hypnotized by the sight of the gun, allowed themselves to be persuaded. But it didn't turn out so badly—Yamamoto put two of Sadako's brothers to work at his Toyo Club.

At first, the Federal Government wasn't interested in the man named Yamamoto—the crimes charged against him were none of Uncle Sam's business; they were matters for the state and city authorities. But in July, 1932, Washington operatives placed his name on their Blacklist—a man to be watched and convicted if possible.

This was the result of the seizure of thirty pounds of morphine which two Japanese tried to smuggle into Seattle aboard the *Venice Maru*, which had just arrived from Kobe, Japan.

The Customs men weren't satisfied merely with convicting the two smugglers; they wanted the higher-ups, too. From feelers they put out in the underworld, they got tips that the dope shipment was to have been delivered to various dope peddlers, but the entire transaction was being financed by a group of Japanese racketeers led by such men as Kanekichi Yamamoto of Seattle and S. Onuma of Tacoma. Altogether, a half-dozen Japs were named. But Customs and Narcotics men tried in vain to get any evidence against them.

Then the Customs ace, Melvin Hanks, suggested a new approach. The smuggled morphine had been packed in 25-ounce tins. The tins all carried the label of a drug factory in Osaka, Japan.

"Let's see if the Japanese authorities will help us," he suggested. "We can send them photos of these tins. Under Japanese law, any factory selling dope has to have a license from their government, and keep records showing who their customers are."

The plan was adopted. Photographs and details were sent to the American Consul at Osaka. He, in turn, wrote a letter to Police Chief Miyata of Osaka, asking for an interview in the matter. He didn't even get an answer. The only thing that happened was that the American authorities found themselves being followed by Japanese secret service men.

This baffled Vice-Consul Edmund Dorsz and Treasury Attaché Martin Scott. They knew that the Japanese Government was behind vast shipments of dope going into the conquered provinces of China—the purpose being to debauch and demoralize the Chinese. But the Americans couldn't see the Japanese being so foolish as to think they could weaken the United States in such a way. What they didn't realize at that time was the astonishing fact that Japan's government wanted its gangsters in America to come to no harm—they were too valuable as collectors of information on our army and navy.

After they had waited several weeks, and there was no reply from Chief Miyata, Scott declared, "I'm going to barge into his office, and make an emphatic request that he help us."

But when he saw Miyata, all he got was politeness and evasion. The police chief said there was nothing he could do—he was very sorry.

"The statements of the Osaka police are all buncombe," Scott reported. "My office is in no position to accomplish any undercover work. With the strict police surveillance that exists, any attempt to do so would only have the most unpleasant reactions. We can, therefore, only rely on the assistance of the local police. As long as this is refused, we are helpless. . . ."

[172]

Meanwhile, the Seattle Customs had arrested a German ship engineer who had been on the fringes of a smuggling venture. To clear himself, he offered to help the government men. He had knocked around the Orient a good deal, and knew the Japanese language.

He was assigned to go to Tacoma and see if the suspect Onuma would sell him some dope—in that way, the Treasury men hoped to catch the Jap red-handed.

"Play them along," Hanks instructed him. "Tell them you want to make connections with them for a morphine ring in New York. But don't let on that you understand the Japanese language."

The informer made contact with Onuma, and was asked to come to a meeting with Onuma and other Japs.

At the session, he offered to buy all the morphine they had. The Japs looked at each other.

Onuma was cautious. "He looks all right, but I think we should check on him a little more," he said in Japanese. In English, he said to the Treasury's man, "Are you ready to pay $80 an ounce?"

The informer appeared to grow angry. "I'll say I'm not! What are you trying to do—rob me? Why, I can get all I want in Portland for $60 an ounce."

The Japs giggled. "Now I know that the white man should be investigated a little more," Onuma said to them in his own language. "He doesn't even know that we're all tied together in one group."

The deal didn't go through, but the informer's information was of utmost value. For the first time, the Customs men became aware that, instead of the usual dope rings operating independently—they were all members of one syndicate. The question was: Who headed the ring?

The Japs all hung together—there was little chance of getting any of them to tattle. So the Treasury agents began shadowing them as well as they could, getting a line on their activities.

As a result, the agents were able to learn of several

shipments due to arrive—the dope was confiscated and several of the smugglers went to the penitentiary. One of them was Onuma, caught red-handed with thirty-five pounds of morphine. He went to the pentitentiary for nine years.

As one after another of the suspects was caught, one kept looming bigger and bigger—the man Yamamoto. It was clear enough now that he wasn't being caught red-handed because he was the boss—he never handled narcotics with his own hands, he was too cunning for that.

Not that there weren't some Japs who wanted Yamamoto caught. They were very tired of always playing the "fall guy."

One day, the Customs got a letter from one of them, a Japanese seaman. It read in part, referring to Yamamoto as "Kinppachi," which in Japanese means the "Big Shot."

Boss of instigator name Kenkichi Yamamoto, popular name Kinppachi, he just now in Los Angeles and is chief Japanese gambling house all western coast of America. He is knave, has always unlawful action, smuggling and inhumanity act and murder. This matter is very perplexing, but I think you take off this Kinppachi, and will stop all unjust action. We are one of seamen to say you—we don't like this hog. He is cruelty and inhumanity more than smuggling. Listen.

Nine years ago, he and friend murder Japanese captain that time the ship docking at Tacoma or Seattle. We must be revenged. They have many affair. Five years ago they killed. . . .

Many people know that Kinppachi is unlawful action against your country but are afraid to tell. Many of your politician are crooked themselves, and when people come to tell about this, they don't do anything about it. Because this Kinppachi is paying to people.

Kinppachi is always going on the airplane to and from Seattle and Los Angeles. If you should search this Japanese you will find pistol on him, you should tell him there is no use for a pistol and ask him why he is carrying one. We wish, concerning this question, the American government hold a strong attitude.

But it was only an anonymous letter, signed, "By one of Japanese seamen." Yamamoto had enemies among the Japanese, but none who dared come into court against him.

In September, 1935, Seattle's shrewd Supervising Agent of Customs, Joseph Green, was authorized to begin a special investigation concentrating on Yamamoto. When asked how long the case might require, Green replied soberly, "At least a year. Little Caesar will give us a plenty hard run for our money."

The investigators tried everything in their bag of tricks. They shadowed the gang overlord on his frequent plane trips of inspection to his various dens; others trailed the automobiles of everybody seen to contact Yamamoto.

But Little Caesar seemed to have inscrutable ways of running his affairs, without being caught. And it seemed that he could smell a stool pigeon a mile away.

Green's hopes rose one day. That was when he got a wire from San Francisco, from an agent who had succeeded in finding a Japanese informer who promised that he'd make a dope deal with Yamamoto.

Decoded, the message ran:

Little Caesar left here by plane at 6: 40 P. M. for Seattle. He and my monkey met for a few minutes and had a nice talk wherein "Stuff" was mentioned plenty. It looks as if we might be in a position in a very short while to get either the bigshot—or a good double-crossing.

As it turned out, the Customs men got neither one nor the other. The informer simply decided he was playing too dangerous a game. Yamamoto's killers had too good a reputation.

It wasn't long before Little Caesar knew that the Treasury men were after him. But he felt himself secure

—so much so that he could even talk frankly with them.

When he ran across an Agent on a Seattle street one day, he said, "Why don't you fellows lay off me?"

"I don't know what you're talking about," the Agent said.

Yamamoto smiled sourly, then he tried to be genial again. "You've got nothing on me. And you're just making me unfriendly. I could be a valuable friend."

"How?"

Yamamoto shrugged. "I could help you get anybody you want. Just tell me who—you can have him either dead or alive."

"I don't doubt it," the Agent said. "But I'm afraid I can't accept the offer. Let's see—how many have you and your thugs killed by now?"

Yamamoto grinned. "That's for you to find out. By the way, I'm going away on a vacation."

The investigation continued turning up many surprising little items. One was that various police officers, all the way from Los Angeles to Seattle, were pals of Kanekichi Yamamoto and his crowd.

Another was that the Japanese colony along our West Coast looked on him as the law. He sold "protection" just as willingly as he sold anything else. One time a Japanese-owned bank failed. Depositors blamed the bank's president, accusing him of having speculated with their funds. They were going to beat him up, or worse.

But when he began appearing around town with a pair of Yamamoto bodyguards at his heels, the irate depositors understood the lay of the land, and let the banker alone.

As for Yamamoto himself, in some way or other, he had managed to have himself made a Deputy Sheriff in Seattle. This gave him the immunity of a law officer's badge and the legal right to carry a gun.

But all this didn't explain how such an out-and-out gangster could be so high up in the Japanese community. Customs agents watched in amazement as nearly every

Japanese diplomat passing the West Coast en route to Washington always looked up Yamamoto, and came to the feasts he threw for them.

It began to make a little more sense, however, one day when a Customs Patrol radio operator at Browning, Montana, intercepted a radio message being sent by short-wave to somebody in Japan. There was heavy static and part of the message was blanked out. But enough was deciphered to indicate clearly that the message concerned American coastal defenses—and the sender was Yamamoto.

A check was made on all amateur radio stations in America and the Hawaiian islands run by Japanese. There turned out to be 125 of them—and it was impossible to determine which had sent the message.

The Customs men's suspicions that Yamamoto was using his gambling clubs not only as headquarters for his racketeers but also for a nest of Japanese spies was confirmed a short while later when they learned that many of the Japanese automobiles they were shadowing were also being tailed by operatives of the American Naval Intelligence.

From entirely different sources, the Customs and the Naval Intelligence had each come to the conclusion that Yamamoto was a master spy. After that, the two outfits kept each other informed as to progress. But Yamamoto seemed to be as cunning a spy, as he was a racket king. Plenty of Japs who hung around our naval bases and airports were seen to frequent his gambling dens, but really conclusive evidence—the kind necessary to convict remained lacking.

It seemed impossible to get an undercover man into the confidence of Yamamoto's gang, in spite of many and ingenious efforts to do so. Yamamoto's spies were apparently so numerous and well-placed that he could keep a close check on the activities of the Federal men. One day a confidential circular was sent out concerning the Yamamoto investigation. It told of the men being shadowed, the license numbers of the cars they were using, etc. It asked all officials concerned to be on the lookout. The circular went to twenty-four offices on our West Coast, Hawaii, and Alaska—to the offices of Narcotics and Customs Agents, Coast Guard, Vice-Consuls, and Collectors of Customs.

A few days later a Naval Intelligence officer came to see Supervising Customs Agent Green in Seattle.

"The Jap crowd has had a bad scare," he said. "They're rid of their cars and using taxis instead. They're taking more precautions than they've used in the past four years."

On top of that, Green was visited by J. P. Wall, Narcotics Bureau Agent-in-Charge at Seattle. He mentioned a name.

"I've never heard of him. But he came to my office yesterday, said he thinks we're investigating him, and says he's going to sue somebody for defaming his character if we don't lay off him. Who is he?"

"Just a crooked cop who has been playing with Yamamoto," said Green. "Don't worry about him—he's just trying to scare us. The boys have evidently been tailing him pretty closely since we put his name on that confidential circular."

It wasn't until March, 1937, that the Federal men saw a real opportunity to smash Yamamoto's power.

That was when Customs Guard T. G. Wallace submitted a report on a long and careful investigation he had been making into the Japanese gambling clubs which operated up and down the West Coast. Here is what he had learned:

In 1906, a group known as the Chinese Highbinders flourished on the West Coast, dealing in all kinds of vice. The gang was eventually stamped out by the police in various cities who began arresting the members on one charge or another, every time they were seen on the streets.

In 1910, a group of Japs organized a similar outfit

specializing in gambling, blackmail, prostitution, smuggling and con games. They catered only to Orientals, and set up branches near the harvest camps, where they could provide women and gambling for Oriental laborers.

The better class of Japanese-Americans tried to stamp out the association of crooks. They held mass meetings to decide on ways to fight the evil. One such meeting was held by the Japanese Association of Oakland, California, one day in 1915. As the association's secretary was walking out of the meeting, he was shot dead by one of the thugs, Tobihei Tominaga.

Although Tominaga was sent to San Quentin Prison, there were a half dozen murders of the same kind in which nobody was caught—and the better-class Japanese had to give up their struggle. By 1915, the crime ring covered the entire West Coast, and even sent gunment to New York City to organize a branch there.

In 1919, the gang incorporated itself at Los Angeles as the "Little Tokyo Social Club of California," and set up branch clubs along the West Coast, known also as "Little Tokyo" clubs.

But their operations smelled to high heaven. In 1930, the better-class Japanese provided the authorities with enough evidence to shut the clubs down—but later, they opened again, the only difference being that from then on, they tried to have a more respectable front.

Each club had its own corps of gunmen who received a regular salary plus a bonus for every person they killed or forced to get out of the city. In ten years, they were responsible for at least eighteen murders known to the authorities—but not one of the murders could be solved.

To the casual passer-by, the clubs seemed nothing more than gambling joints. But each maintained a lookout across the street to warn of approaching police, through use of a buzzer. And each was a rendezvous for Japanese gangsters and spies. The latter were always visiting Japanese ships which came into port, in order to send telegrams back to Japan—not caring to let their messages be read by employees of American cable companies.

But on the surface, the clubs seemed to be only places where Orientals gathered to play blackjack, stud and draw poker, fan-tan and Japanese dominoes. The clubs enforced their own brand of law. Any Japanese seen gambling in a Chinese joint was marked for death.

In June, 1930, there began a series of murders which threw the clubs into confusion. The bloody business began when Yoshiaki Yasuda, president of the "Little Tokyo" club at Los Angeles, was shot dead by two Orientals in front of his home. The killing was witnessed by Yasuda's wife and two members of his bodyguard. But they wouldn't talk to police about it. The police had to learn for themselves, a short while later, that the murderer had been one of Yasuda's erstwhile pals, Sego Nojiri, in charge of the club's white-slavers. It had been a feud over a money debt.

A few weeks later, Nojiri himself was found full of bullet holes in "Japanese Alley." Murders began tumbling upon each other, as the feud spread. That was when Yamamoto entered the scene with his own gunmen, declaring that from now on there was going to be peace and tranquillity. He was going to take care of all the dirty work; the clubs should confine themselves to gambling. And from this gambling in return for keeping the peace, he was to get a cut of the profits.

It was this investigation that gave the Federal men their clue. They knew it was practically impossible to convict Yamamoto of murder, or espionage, or dope smuggling or any other such crime requiring Japanese witnesses. The Japs were too scared of the gangster to testify.

But—Yamamoto must be making himself a big pile of money. And like all gangsters of his type, he was undoubtedly "forgetting" to pay his income taxes. A quick checkup revealed this conjecture to be correct. The Internal Revenue Bureau was getting no taxes from Kane-kichi Yamamoto.

That was when the Customs men were joined by Intelligence Unit officers of the Treasury. They visited the various gambling dens owned by Yamamoto, as well as those he was "protecting" and came away with all records. Then they began prowling through the gang king's bank accounts, living costs—a long, careful checkup on his financial status.

Meanwhile, on April 2nd, 1937, the Japanese steamer *Heian Maru* docked at Seattle. Among her passengers was one Seiihci Tensaka, whom a Customs man immediately recognized as being on the smuggler Blacklist—a henchman of Yamamoto.

Customs Agent George W. Harlow led a squad to look over Tensaka's luggage. Nothing suspicious was found.

"But Tensaka looks a little jittery to me," said Harlow. " I wonder why."

Then they discovered that the same vessel had brought in some freight shipped by Tensaka. It consisted of 100 small tubs labeled as containing soy-bean sauce.

Harlow took out the bung of one of the tubs, and poked a stick down into it. The stick went down all the way—there was obviously no false bottom, or anything like that. When the stick came out, it was dripping with brown soy-bean sauce.

Harlow tried three more tubs, with the same result. Then he tried a fifth. This time, the stick went down only half-way.

The Customs men quickly ripped off the top of the tub, and poured out the liquid. As they had suspected, they found a false bottom. It was pulled up. Upon the real bottom of the tub, they found a thin container, just large enough to fill the space beneath the false bottom.

And inside the tin, they found three pounds of morphine—along with bundles of closely packed nails. The nails had been put in the tub to even up the weight, so this tub would not be suspiciously lighter than those full of sauce. Before the sleuths were through testing tubs that day, they had discovered four more containing dope in the same way.

Tensaka's arrest in itself wasn't as significant as what followed.

"Better hurry over to those Customs people," Consul Okamoto told Yamamoto. "They've caught your friend Tensaka, and it looks bad."

Sure enough, Little Caesar quickly appeared at the Customs Office, asking if there was anything he could do to straighten matters.

He insisted on speaking to Tensaka. Supervising Agent Green, burly and slowspoken, had been waiting for just such a request. He had already asked Agent Willard Kingsbury to be around—Kingsbury understood the Japanese language.

Green acted reluctant, but finally allowed Yamamoto to see his henchman.

"What's happened?" Yamamoto quickly asked Tensaka in Japanese.

The latter shrugged, "I got caught—that's all. But there's more coming—with the ship's doctor on the N. Y. K. Line, on their next boat."

Yamamoto was staring at Kingsbury. Then he turned quickly to Tensaka, "Shut up! Don't talk any more."

He turned, and rushed from the room.

"They tricked us," he told the Consul. "They had an agent there who understands Japanese—I'm sure of it, by the way he was listening. And Tensaka talked too much. He told about the ship's doctor."

"Oh, oh," replied Okamoto sorrowfully.

"Yes, and you better see the N. Y. K. people right away and get them to warn the doctor. It wouldn't do for the Americans to catch the doctor—he's too important, as you know. So get right to work on it."

Consult Okamoto came the next day, full of hissing politeness and accompanied by his stenographer, to Supervising Agent Green's office.

"I should like," he said, "to ask you several things about this Tensaka affair, to find out what are the facts."

Green leaned back in his chair a moment, then said, "That's a strange request! I haven't even made a full report to my own government yet."

"But," said Okamoto, with a fawning smile, "I wish to cooperate, you see."

"Yes," Green muttered. "I see. Well, look here. I see you've brought along your stenographer. Suppose I call in mine. Then you ask your questions. And then—I'll have a few to ask you, Mr. Okamoto."

The Consult got up and put on his hat. "I'm afraid we do not understand each other," he said angrily.

"I'm afraid we don't. Goodby!"

Tensaka was convicted and sent to McNeil Island Penitentiary. And, of course, the mysterious Jap ship's doctor never darkened our shores with his presence. But the Customs had learned once again that the Japanese Government was standing behind its smugglers—and there could be only one reason for that. The smugglers brought in dope and took back espionage reports.

Meanwhile, other Treasury men had been sweating over Yamamoto's financial setup. He banked his money in Los Angeles, in Seattle, in Yokohama. His accounts were under dozens of aliases. Two accounts were in his wife's name. Another was in the name of his bookkeeper. In his own name, in a Seattle bank, he had the tidy sum of $250,000.

There was plenty of evidence to convict him of income tax evasion, and the order went out to bring him in.

Agents found him at his Toyo Club. He came along cockily, confident that this was one rap he would beat. But he didn't like the looks of things when his deputy Sheriff's badge and gun were taken away from him, and he found himself in jail under $25,000 bail.

"We can fix it some way," he pleaded. "I'll pay every cent you claim that I owe—if you don't send me to the pen."

The Japanese Government sent over no less a personage than Shinji Taniguchi, Inspector of the Tokyo Police.

Yamamoto was out on bail, and there was no law to prevent him from talking to anybody he wanted—but Taniguchi nevertheless asked Agent Hanks for "permission" to see Yamamoto.

A few days later, he looked up Hanks again. "I have arranged everything," he said. "Mr. Yamamoto is willing to talk the case over with you."

"That's all right with me," Hanks said, "but I'm promising him nothing. Anything he says may later be used against him."

"I'm sure we can fix everything," Taniguchi said. "The Japanese government would like this closed."

With three other Treasury men, to listen in as witnesses, Hanks went on October 3rd, 1937, to Inspector Taniguchi's hotel room in Los Angeles. Yamamoto was there. Inspector Taniguchi locked the door, and told Yamamoto to proceed.

"I want to help you fight the narcotics traffic," said Little Caesar.

"But you've been head of the racket," Hanks said.

Yamamoto shrugged. "Don't misunderstand me. You haven't smuggling evidence against me. What I want to do is help you convict others. I'm not a stool pigeon—I'm making this offer because my government wants me out of this jam."

"I understand," Hanks said. "You've lived here over twenty years, but you still consider Japan your country."

"Certainly. I'm very loyal to the Mikado. My government has reasons for wanting me freed. That is why I make my offer. I am the law among Japanese in America. I will turn over to you any smugglers you want. I will forbid smuggling. And any Japanese who violates my order—you, Mr. Hanks, will not have to prosecute. I will have him delivered in a sack to your office door—all you will have to do is bury him!"

Of course, Hanks declined to make any bargain.

We didn't have enough evidence to convict Yamamoto of espionage, or of smuggling, but the Treasury was convinced it had Little Caesar squirming in an income tax trap. And Yamamoto went to trial.

The Treasury men didn't pretend that they had uncovered all of Yamamoto's earnings. But they had found enough to figure that he owed Uncle Sam the sum of $28,711.37. Not having paid it, he was guilty of tax fraud. That was the verdict of the jury, and Little Caesar—just a little shot again—was led off to serve a term of one and a half years at McNeil Island Penitentiary.

Before he could come out, he had to pay the money he owed, plus a $3,000 fine. And even then, Uncle Sam wasn't through with him. Prison guards didn't take their handcuffs off him until he was aboard the *Hie Maru*—along with his wife and children—bound for Japan, forbidden ever to return to this country.

"I like it here in America," Yamamoto explained to one of his guards, "but your government doesn't like me."

But the war gangsters running Japan didn't share this dislike for a criminal.

They put him right to work. The Treasury got proof of this a year later when our operatives caught two of Yamamoto's agents trying to smuggle strategic war materials out of this country. Still trying to carry on his spy work.

THE END